HOW TO DIE AND LIVE TO TELL ABOUT IT

BECKY BARTNESS

HOW TO DIE AND LIVE TO TELL ABOUT IT

iUniverse books may be ordered through booksellers or by contacting:

iUniverse
1663 Liberty Drive
Bloomington, IN 47403
www.iuniverse.com
1-800-Authors (1-800-288-4677)

ISBN: 978-1-4917-4878-7 (sc)
ISBN: 978-1-4917-4879-4 (e)

Library of Congress Control Number: 2014917546

Printed in the United States of America.

iUniverse rev. date: 11/18/2014

CHAPTER 1

Following the lead of a self-help book I picked up in the sales aisle of Changing Hands Book Store, I took the first step toward becoming the new Kate Williams—a prosperous, better-built, and well-balanced woman. Goal number one was a new house, consistent with the theory that new beginnings required new surroundings.

That was how I came to die.

But I'm getting ahead of myself. First, I have to tell you about the aliens.

CHAPTER 2

I am an attorney by training and inclination. I am five feet eight inches tall and have dark blonde hair. Some people have compared my looks to those of Christie Brinkley. I always respond that I'd rather have Christie's money than her looks.

After fourteen years of practice in Chicago, I decided to relocate to Phoenix, Arizona, and adopt a saner lifestyle by cutting down on my hours and developing a social life. A year and a half after my move, I have my own law firm in a converted cottage in downtown Phoenix and employ a staff of three: Beth, my sixty-four-year-old half-Kenyan and half-Italian secretary; Sam, my fashion-conscious investigator with a penchant for high heels and other men; and MJ, my fashion-unconscious paralegal who expresses herself with tattoos the way some people load their cars with bumper stickers. I even have two boyfriends: Bryan Turner, whose status is reduced to part-time boyfriend while he campaigns for the position of sheriff—Bryan is currently serving as interim sheriff—and Mark Ramos, a twenty-five-year-old personal trainer who looks like a young Brad Pitt.

I am also the proud owner of Ralph, a large dog of indeterminate breed who is an overachiever in the areas of shedding and drooling, and a cat I call Her, a name that causes endless confusion.

To complete this picture of paranormalcy, add Tuwanda, my best friend and client; my seventy-eight-year-old neighbor, Macy, a retired Realtor from Brooklyn for whom food is a major coping mechanism; another neighbor, Cal, who is a cross-dressing retired FBI agent; a couple of homeless guys; and a ghost whisperer—and there you have the primary players in my life.

Of these, Tuwanda was the most directly responsible for my death.

I'd like to use a dissonance between the mundane beginning of the week and an ensuing climax to build dramatic tension here, but I can't because the week began lousy and stayed lousy, except the intensity of the lousiness increased.

My real-estate agent, Jane Hendricks, had scheduled several house viewings for that Monday. The plan was to meet at a local restaurant, review the portfolio Jane had compiled, and then commence the touring.

I was referred to Jane by a passing acquaintance. Based on my prior experience with real-estate agents, excluding Macy, who is unremittingly honest, I knew I was dealing with a category of individuals whose insincerity was unmatched except perhaps by that of politicians and my attorney colleagues. That being the case, one was as good or as bad as another, so I didn't invest much energy in the selection process.

Thus far, I'd spoken to Jane only over the phone. All my preconceived notions of real-estate agents had been proven correct by the end of our conversation. When I gave her my price range, she immediately suggested several homes on the market for double my budget. After I demurred, she tried to appeal to my vanity by mentioning that a person of my stature should consider only high-end neighborhoods.

I'm a criminal defense attorney, and the local rag's stock photo of me is a picture of me running naked from a house fire while holding a Chihuahua. I have no illusions as to my stature in the community. A PR agent I hired was making headway in the image department, but she had lots of negative press to undo.

I asked Tuwanda to come along on the house tour because I greatly valued her opinion. She knew me better than anyone, with the possible exception of Bryan, and had lived in Phoenix all her life.

Tuwanda accepted the invitation but begged off on breakfast, agreeing to meet us at the restaurant once we were ready to leave on the house tour. (She lived only a few blocks away.)

I met Jane at a trendy local eatery known for its excellent omelets and poor service. The high-school kid waiting on us asked me to repeat my order for a Swiss cheese omelet while she laboriously wrote it out in longhand. The kitchen staff subsequently translated the order as eggs Benedict. Jane's dry wheat toast and coffee came out as orange juice and a breakfast burrito. Neither of us complained when the food arrived, though, because we were on a tight schedule.

As she handed me sheets of sales information, Jane briefly described the houses we were visiting. Her perfectly coiffed, shoulder-length blonde hair did not move despite the exaggerated body language she used to convey enthusiasm for each of the properties. She spoke with the tenor of a cheerleader hardwired for being perky and looked as if she had disregarded the warnings about tanning beds.

My own dark-blonde hair had not seen the inside of a beauty salon in weeks.

"This one is my absolute favorite," Jane gushed for the umpteenth time as she passed me the photo of another overpriced house. "It has a six-car garage and a helicopter pad."

"I have one car and no helicopters," I said flatly. I did not add that I disliked helicopters, having had an unfortunate experience with one recently. "My only requirements are three bedrooms and a fenced yard for Ralph."

"But this one is more than nine thousand square feet and has *ten* bedrooms. You could use the helicopter pad as a play court or as an entertainment area. Just think of the wonderful parties you could have."

I did not see anything festive about a helicopter pad.

"I don't need more than twenty-five hundred square feet. I wouldn't know what to do with a larger house."

"A larger house is great for entertaining," enthused Jane.

Why was this woman fixated on entertaining? To my way of thinking, a home is a place of refuge, not a place where you add to the stress of living by taking on the duties of hostess.

That's not to say I'm antisocial. Part of the reason I wanted to move was that my one-bedroom condo was not large enough for a lifestyle that includes dog sleepovers (Tuwanda's dog, Walter, is a frequent overnight guest), two boyfriends, a best friend who treats my home as her own, and the occasional emergency guest.

Jane sighed as she pulled a laptop out of her capacious purse and proceeded to rapidly tap keys with long, perfectly manicured nails whose light lilac paint complemented the purple in her Tory Burch suit. She'd shoved her barely touched breakfast burrito toward me to make room for her computer, which I took as an invitation to share.

"Should we reschedule for another day then?" I asked through a mouthful of scrambled eggs and tortilla.

"No," she answered. "Give me a few seconds with my phone and laptop, and we'll be set."

I had to hand it to her. She had a new schedule in place by the time I finished her burrito.

"Your square-footage limitation eliminates some of the better neighborhoods, but I think you'll still be pleased with the selection. Are you ready to get started, Kate? You may ride with me if you'd like. That way, you can look around and check out the neighborhoods as we pass through."

I explained that I'd invited a friend to join us. Jane assured me an extra person would not be a problem since her car had lots of room.

While I called Tuwanda on my cell, Jane went to the ladies room to freshen up just in time to miss the bill. I paid, adding a 20 percent tip even though in a just world, our waitress should have paid *me*. (I felt sorry for her because I too had been a waitress in high school, and it was a tough gig.)

Jane joined me on the curb in front of the restaurant, and in under a minute, Tuwanda pulled into a nearby parking space.

Jane's eyes widened when she saw Tuwanda's ride: a pink 1983 El Dorado Cadillac convertible, heavy on the chrome, with spinners and dual exhausts. Billy Joel's "Uptown Girl" blared from a state-of-the-art sound system, and the car's raised top and closed windows did nothing to muffle its volume.

Jane added an open mouth to her wide eyes when Tuwanda got out of the car. Tuwanda, who is owner and manager of Pole Polishers, a local house of prostitution, was still in her business clothes even though her workday is usually over by five o'clock in the morning. She looked like a black Angelina Jolie and was wearing a pink Chanel sheath with matching Jimmy Choos.

"Long day?" I asked.

"Damn right. One of my Care Bares got beat up by her two o'clock appointment. JJ and me had to go pay him a visit and straighten him out on the rules."

The Care Bares were Pole Polishers' service staff. JJ, a retired professional football player, was in charge of Pole Polishers' security and collection department, which consisted of him.

"Is she going to be okay?" I asked.

"Yeah, she gonna be fine. I gave her a couple days off to recover from the psychological trauma, though."

"Is her client going to be all right?" I asked.

She shrugged. "When we left, he was curled up in the corner of his hotel room, whimperin', so it was hard to tell."

Tuwanda jerked her head toward Jane. "Is *she* gonna be all right?"

Jane had turned ashen and was visibly shaking. Her faux bonhomie had been put to the test, and it had failed her.

"Are you okay to drive, Jane?" I asked. "My car's not big enough for the three of us, but I'm sure Tuwanda wouldn't mind if we took her car."

Faced with this threat, Jane took a moment to regroup.

"No, no, no. I'm fine," she insisted, but she didn't sound convincing.

I belatedly introduced the two women after we were seated in Jane's late-model BMW.

I took the front passenger seat, and Tuwanda sat in the back. I turned and looked at her with a raised eyebrow.

"Don't worry. I ain't gonna take a nap," she said.

Tuwanda views most backseat travel as an opportunity to catch forty winks, and I needed her to pay attention.

Jane adjusted the rear-view mirror to block out her view of Tuwanda, probably based on the "out of sight, out of mind" theory. Whatever the reason, it seemed to calm her.

As she drove, she rattled off a list of prestigious golf clubs, expensive restaurants, and malls in the area we were heading to. She characterized its population as wealthy and well educated, the implication being that these were my kind of people.

I could feel waves of distaste emanating from the backseat.

"The first house we're going to visit," she said, "is in North Scottsdale, and—"

"Uh-uh," interrupted Tuwanda. "Tha's too far out, an' them people up there is soulless, superficial snobs. They spend they time golfin' on private golf courses, gettin' plastic surgery, an' shoppin' for shit they don't need."

"I live in North Scottsdale," Jane said frostily.

"Your point bein'?"

Let me mention here that normally Tuwanda is polite to people she's just met, but she was tired, and Jane's elitist rhetoric had gotten to her. Tuwanda has no patience for pretension.

Jane made a series of little huffing noises.

"You don't know me well enough to judge," she said once the huffing stopped. "For instance, I am part of a professional women's organization that, last year, raised more than $2,000 so underprivileged children could take sailing lessons."

"You tellin' me you raised money so kids with lousy schools who go to their lousy schools hungry most days can learn how to sail boats in a state that's mostly desert?"

Jane said nothing but made more huffing noises.

"Wait a minute," said Tuwanda. "You say this organization is for professional women? Hell, I'm a professional woman. Maybe I can join and help out with your charitable givin' plan."

Jane remained mute, but her struggle against self-expression was palpable. Her flexing jaw muscles indicated serious teeth grinding. I wouldn't have been surprised if she'd started foaming at the mouth. She managed to fight back the instinct to show real emotion, however, and her veneer of professionalism slid back into place.

"You would be a fantastic asset to our organization, I'm sure," she chirped. "But I'm guessing you live in South Phoenix, and our membership is only open to residents of North Scottsdale."

Jane's reference to South Phoenix was a thinly veiled comment about Tuwanda's race. A large percentage of Phoenix's black population still lived in South Phoenix, which, before the age of political correctness, would have been called a ghetto. Today politicians refer to it as a redevelopment opportunity.

"What you mean by that?" growled Tuwanda.

"I think we should forget about North Scottsdale. I need to be closer to my office," I said hastily. "What other areas do you suggest?"

Jane made a big show of making a U-turn and headed south.

"I have listings in Paradise Valley, Arcadia, and Encanto I would like to show you," she said. Half-turning to Tuwanda, she added, "That is, if it's okay with you, Teresa."

"Tuwanda," corrected Tuwanda.

"Tuwanda," repeated Jane. "What an interesting name. Is it a family name?"

"I don't know. Could be. When my people was ripped out of Africa to work as slaves in this country, no one bothered to find out what they names was. Plantation records list my great-great-great-great-great granddaddy as John, property of

Robert MacKay. At some point, my family got tired of writin' *Propertyofrobertmackay* as they last name, so they started usin' Jones. My momma named me Tuwanda cuz it sounded African. Turns out *Tuwanda* means 'bear' in Goshute, but that works too since my ancestors picked up some Native American blood somewhere along the way."

Jane stopped asking Tuwanda questions and instead mined me for information in a fruitless effort to bond.

We eventually pulled into the driveway of a newish pink-stucco house in a style that looked like a cross between Spanish and Italian, although the freestanding garage reflected a Bauhaus influence. It would have had curb appeal only to a schizophrenic.

"No," I said simply.

"Hell no," added Tuwanda.

We backed out of the driveway and then continued to head south.

The second house was in Arcadia, an area formerly dominated by citrus orchards and now populated by lovely ranch-style houses built in the fifties and newer McMansions built by wealthy professionals who appreciated the area's central location. The house we went to fell into the former category. From the outside, it looked warm and inviting with its large lawn, painted white brick and wood exterior, and dark green shutters. It was located on a small cul-de-sac, and the surrounding houses were of similar style and vintage.

"The house is on lockbox, so we can take our time looking around without inconveniencing the owners," said Jane. She hesitated, resting her hand on the ignition key, but hearing nothing negative from her passengers, she cut the engine and got out. Motioning for us to stay in the car, she walked to the front door to deal with the lockbox.

"I like the looks of this place," I commented to Tuwanda.

"It's got promise," said Tuwanda. "But don't say nothin' to that real-estate agent. If she thinks you like it, she won't try to get the price down. If she thinks you could go either way, she'll try harder."

Jane had the door open, and she signaled for us to join her.

The good feeling I got from the outside of the house continued into its interior. The door opened into an airy foyer overlooking a comfortable family room. Through a solid wall of French doors, a verdant backyard with a flagstone patio, stone fireplace, and kidney-shaped pool was visible.

I looked at the sales sheet Jane had given me and was amazed that the list price was almost within my budget. If there was wiggle room, a purchase was doable.

Jane led us to the kitchen, pointing out the upgraded appliances and gourmet stove, all of which meant nothing to me. All I needed was a refrigerator and a microwave.

The home had two smaller bedrooms joined by a reasonably large bathroom, but the pièce de résistance was the master suite. My entire condo could have fit in it. The room had a dynamite view of the backyard, and the attached bathroom had a walk-in snail shower and a huge bathtub with a whirlpool feature. The closet was large enough to accommodate my present wardrobe, with lots of space left over that I would have to buy clothes to fill because nature abhors a vacuum.

I wanted this house. I wanted it bad.

Per Tuwanda's advice, I maintained a neutral expression despite my tap-dancing inner self, and I asked casual questions about the area, which I already knew well because it was a mere five minutes by car from my present home.

"Why'd the people who lived here leave?" asked Tuwanda.

Jane patted her perfect hair, a move I was beginning to recognize as a prelude to serious finessing.

"The owners live out of state. I understand there was an unfortunate accident, and the wife wanted to move."

"What kind of unfortunate accident?" Tuwanda said.

"A child drowned in the pool, an occurrence that is all too common in Phoenix," said Jane as if pointing out a patch of crabgrass.

Jane's statement triggered memories of the skeleton of a child found under the floor of my office, and I had a terrible thought: What if I was only attracted to properties associated with tragedy?

"Of course, there's a good chance that any house more than twenty years old is going to have some sort of sadness associated with it. That's how life works," chirped Jane. "Now let's have a look at the backyard."

The tragic story of the child's drowning had tamped down my enthusiasm, but I followed her through the back door nonetheless.

The yard was beautiful, even in its overgrown state. The flagstone patio was larger than it had appeared from inside and was surrounded by flowering plants. Two flagstone steps led down to the pool area and a flagstone pool surround. The rest of the yard was grass except for a grouping of Aleppo pines in a back corner. The fence enclosing the yard was too high for even Ralph the wonder dog to jump.

As I strolled around, I spotted four round holes worn into the grass—the imprint of a child's swing set. I felt a sudden, deep sadness and then looked around nervously.

By way of explanation, I am semiconvinced that the spirit of the little girl whose skeleton was found under our office building still manifests itself every so often by provoking the building's inhabitants to engage in atypical behavior. The possibility that a spirit inhabited this backyard as well was real to me.

I don't know what I expected to find—spirits, if they exist, are invisible. But I kept an open mind in case a spirit tried to communicate.

Out of the corner of my eye, I caught movement in one of the Aleppos' middle branches. "Who or what is that?" I asked, pointing to the tree.

Jane glanced in the direction I was pointing. "I don't see anything," she said. "Let's go back and take another look at the house's interior."

Tuwanda, who had been inspecting a built-in grill next to the patio, walked to where I was standing and squinted at the tree.

"I think Kate's referrin' to the guy in the swimmin' trunks."

"He's probably just the gardener," said Jane without looking. "Let's head back into the house. I don't think you saw the powder room yet."

"Gardeners don't normally wear bathin' suits, and as a rule, they got gardenin' tools if they messin' around with trees."

I walked to the base of the tree and peered into its branches.

"Hellooo," I called out. "I'm sorry to bother you, sir, but do you work here?"

I received no answer.

Tuwanda repeated the question with doubled volume.

Again, there was no answer.

"You think he's dead?" asked Tuwanda.

"That's absurd," said Jane. "This is a very good neighborhood."

Tuwanda harrumphed. "People die in good neighborhoods too. Besides, you don't know who you dealin' with. Katie here finds bodies all the time. She can't go for a damn walk without findin' a body."

"I'm going to call 911," I said, taking out my cell phone.

"She got it on speed dial," Tuwanda informed Jane.

I shot her a narrow-eyed look while I punched in the number.

I explained the situation in concise terms to the woman who answered, and I waited until she contacted dispatch and then got back on the line.

"Hell, Kate. Maybe we should just follow you around. It would probably save time."

"Who's this?"

"Lorraine."

Lorraine is an ex-Care Bare who began working for the Phoenix Police Department after completing training at the South Phoenix academy. Lorraine picked up my 911 call when I found the body of a rock star while out jogging last month.

Lorraine and I talked for a while, bringing each other up to date on what we'd been doing. Lorraine was taking a quilting class. I had just found another body. Then Tuwanda took the phone from me and chatted for a while with her former employee.

In the meantime, the man in the tree remained silent and immobile.

The faint sound of a siren grew louder and then stopped. No one moved.

"I think that may be the EMTs. Maybe you should go meet them and bring them back here, Jane," I said.

She made an impatient noise and looked at her watch. "This had better not take long." Looking at me as if it were my fault, she added, "You may enjoy this sort of thing, but *I* don't have the time for it."

She trotted off to let in the emergency response team, while I struggled to come up with a snappy retort.

"Not funny!" I finally yelled at her retreating back.

Jane returned, followed by three men in firemen's gear. As they drew nearer, I pointed mutely to the man and the tree, figuring the situation was self-explanatory.

One of the men enquired about additional access to the backyard, and Jane showed them to a gate.

The men disappeared and then reappeared moments later with a ladder. They propped the ladder against the tree, and two of them held it while the third climbed up.

Once he was within reach, he prodded the tree man's leg with a forefinger.

The man harrumphed indignantly and took a swipe at the fireman's head. The fireman, a highly trained professional, yelped and said, "What the hell?" He quickly climbed down. Once earthbound and at a safe distance, he halfheartedly attempted to interrogate the man.

"Who are you, and why are you in this tree?"

"Who are you, and why were *you* in this tree?" countered the tree man.

"I am Captain Peters. We received a call that a person in a tree appeared unresponsive."

"I was meditating, dammit."

"Sir, you are on property that does not belong to you. Please come down."

"No. I've been climbing this tree to meditate for years. I've got rights based on adverse possession."

Captain Peters looked at Jane. "Is this true?"

"I don't know. I'm a real-estate agent. Ask her," she said, pointing to me. "She's an attorney."

Captain Peters shifted his attention to me.

I shrugged. "I don't know all the facts, so I can't offer you an opinion. I'm looking for a house. I just want to find a nice house," I added defensively.

Peters looked around. "Except for the guy in the tree, this is really a nice place," he commented.

We heard the gate open and turned to see who was joining our little discussion group. A uniformed police officer approached us.

I recognized him immediately as Officer Percival Guilford, a.k.a. Bubba, whom I met when he was assigned to guard my condo after the first time a client tried to kill me.

He nodded to me and then asked Captain Peters for a status report.

After Peters finished a brief update, Jane, whose frequent glances at her watch resembled a facial tic, demanded that Bubba arrest the tree man.

"Ma'am, I can't do that as long as there's a valid dispute over property rights, and none of you can assure me that isn't the case," explained Bubba.

Everyone turned to me, and I reluctantly nodded in agreement.

Jane interrupted her watch-watching routine and fixed Bubba with an indignant glare. "So you're just going to let him stay up there?"

"He doesn't appear to be a threat. If that changes, give us a call and we'll come back."

Jane shook her head disgustedly and looked at her watch, which had likely missed the attention.

Bubba and Captain Peters and his crew left, and Jane announced that we too needed to depart a.s.a.p. because the house we were visiting next was occupied, and the owner was waiting.

I hesitated, though, because despite its drawbacks, I liked this house and wanted to pursue the issue of whether the tree man was a permanent fixture.

Returning to the base of the tree, I looked up at him.

"Now that the police and firemen are gone, will you tell me who you are?"

He gave no response. The tree man had gone mute again.

I planted a foot on a lower branch and hoisted myself up. The limbs were sturdy and nicely spaced for climbing. I could see why the tree man had chosen this tree.

I continued to climb, despite Jane's protestations, until I was even with the tree man. I sat on a limb near his, letting my legs dangle and feeling a remembered childhood excitement of freedom and derring-do.

I did not say anything at first but studied him carefully. He was older than he'd appeared from below. The face under the longish gray hair was lined. Even though his body was on the thin side, he looked to be in fairly good shape. His nose was long and pointed and overshadowed a small mouth and nearly nonexistent chin. One of his bright blue eyes was fixed on me, while the other stared obliquely into the distance.

Balancing carefully on my branch, I held out my hand. "I'm Kate Williams."

He looked at me distrustfully with his one focused eye and then slowly extended his hand and gave me a one-pump handshake.

"Nelsen Nelsen," he said.

His parents had either a great sense of humor or a complete lack of originality.

"Having the same first and last names makes it easy to remember," I quipped.

"They're not the same. It's N-e-l-s-e-n N-e-l-s-e-n."

I nodded seriously, as if letting the distinction sink in.

"Have you been swimming?" I asked, nodding toward his swim trunks.

"No. I don't swim. It's hot out, so I dress light."

I could certainly understand that. Phoenix temperatures in September were still in the hundreds.

"Did you know the family that lived here before?" I asked.

He seemed surprised by the question. "In the tree?"

"No, in the house down there," I clarified.

He shook his head. "They seemed nice, though. They didn't mind me sitting in their tree. Sometimes the mother would give me snacks."

I waited a few beats before asking my next question while maintaining the casual tone of our conversation. "When did you start coming up here?"

Of course, his answer would tell me whether he really had a valid claim of adverse possession, since the concept is largely dependent on how long the claimant has used the land without protest by the owner.

Nelsen's answer was immediate. "Since I was abducted."

"So you've been here nonstop since your abduction?"

Nelsen looked at me with concern. "Are you right in the head?"

I struggled to find a response that was both honest and brief.

Fortunately, Nelsen kept going without waiting for an answer.

"I was abducted about eighteen years ago after I climbed this tree to get a better look at the weird lights in the sky. I lived next door, and the yards weren't fenced then. This was—and still is—the best climbing tree in the neighborhood. If I'd been in this tree for eighteen years, I'd be dead. Those weird lights were in all the newspapers, you know. So was the story of my abduction."

Although I had a sinking feeling that I knew the answer, I asked, "Who abducted you?"

"Aliens. Like I said, it was in all the papers. People still talk about it. Rosemarie Putnam demanded that the government investigate, but as usual, they haven't done a damn thing."

Rosemarie Putnam is a Phoenix city councilwoman who, despite her claims of UFO sightings, is returned to office each term by her loyal South Phoenix constituency.

"If this is where you were abducted, why do you come back? Aren't you afraid you'll be abducted again?"

"I want them to take me. They were nice. They gave me my own room and everything."

I looked down at the lovely home and sighed. It was not to be. I could not live in the house with Nelsen sitting in the tree and waiting to be reabducted.

Then I felt a glimmer of hope. "How often do you come up here to wait for the, er, aliens?" I asked, hoping I was using the politically correct term for little green men.

I reasoned that if his tree climbing was no more than an annual pilgrimage, I could deal with it.

"Ten in the morning until noon and then ten p.m. to midnight. I was abducted at eleven p.m., but I figure I should allow for time differences—you know, extraterrestrial daylight savings time and such."

"Then why do you come from ten to noon?"

He shrugged. "Nothin' on TV."

I looked longingly at the lovely patio. Maybe it wouldn't be so bad. I would be either working or sleeping most days during Nelsen's tree time. Heck, Ralph might even enjoy the company. Weekend backyard barbecues with my friends wouldn't be a problem since all of my friends have set a high bar when it comes to weirdness.

"If I move into this house, don't expect me to bring you snacks," I said. "And no littering."

Nelsen nodded seriously, and we shook hands to seal the deal.

I lowered myself to the ground and, after a brief search, found Tuwanda and Jane sitting on the front steps. Neither was speaking, and Jane was still carrying on with her watch.

"Learn anything useful?" asked Tuwanda.

I summarized what Nelsen had told me.

"No way! I remember that! It was a big deal. Half the people in Phoenix swore they saw a UFO hoverin' in the sky. People in Tucson saw it too. Even the guy who was governor then said he saw it, and he was a pale white man with no sense of humor. I remember bein' mad because I was workin' that night and missed all the action."

Jane looked up from her watch, suddenly interested.

"I've heard about that. It happened in 1997, right? People still talk about it. I was living in Los Angeles at the time, but it was all over the national and local news. The incident is still included in every UFO TV special. Even coming from Chicago, Kate, I can't believe you haven't heard about it."

"I avoid anything having to do with outer space and extraterrestrials," I said. "I have enough problems with earthlings."

I headed for Jane's car, determined to drop the topic. It was not to be. As soon as we were on the road, Tuwanda started up again.

"You hear about them aliens abductin' people and probin' 'em. Did Nelsen look like he'd been probed?"

"How does someone look like he's been probed?" I asked.

"Uncomfortable-like when they sit. Kinda shiftin' from side to side."

"Remember that guy who was abducted in northern Arizona?" Jane said. "He said he wasn't probed at all. In fact, he said it was kind of a pleasant experience being abducted and wanted to do it again."

"Maybe they probed in the old days, but now they got better technology so they can just take a picture or somethin'."

"If they're nice, I wouldn't mind being abducted. They couldn't be worse than the assholes who hang out in the Scottsdale bars."

"I agree with that. All them guys want to do is probe."

The conversation had taken a disturbing turn, but at least Jane and Tuwanda were getting along.

The next house was in the Encanto area, a charming oasis near downtown Phoenix with a park and golf course surrounded by lovely homes built in the twenties and thirties—historic monuments, by Phoenix standards.

We pulled up in front of a brick English Tudor-style minimansion with a lush yard surrounded by tall shrubs. The real-estate agent representing the owner met us at the curb and greeted us by saying, "It's about time. Mrs. Goldfein and her children have been circling the block, waiting for the showing to end so they can get back in their home."

I was not sympathetic. We weren't *that* late. If people don't like the inconvenience of having their house shown, then they shouldn't list it for sale.

Jane introduced the real-estate agent as Marva Gordon, and as we followed her into the house, she let loose with a Billy Mays-type spiel.

The home was lovely and had been updated without the loss of the original style. But odd though this may sound, I didn't get the feeling the house needed me. A lovely family would buy it, and it would continue its stately existence with no bumps in the road. The Arcadia house, however, was empty and lonely, with a sad history and a tree man. It needed someone to love it and take care of it, and under the circumstances, it couldn't be too choosey, so it wouldn't mind someone like me.

That's not to say I have low self-esteem. I'm just realistic about who I am and the friends and lifestyle I've chosen.

CHAPTER 3

I thanked Mrs. Gordon politely, and on the way back to the restaurant, I made no comment to Jane about which, if either, home I preferred. As she dropped us off, she promised to get back to me to see how I felt about the homes we'd seen and to schedule additional showings.

Tuwanda wanted a bite to eat, so we found a seat in the restaurant I'd eaten in earlier. After she ordered, we settled in to discuss the house issue.

I presented my opinion of the pros and cons of each house while Tuwanda consumed two omelets and a ham sandwich—she'd ordered only the sandwich but didn't complain when the other food came too. When I finished talking, Tuwanda folded her hands on the table and looked at me somberly.

"This here's a big decision, Katie. I can tell by the way you been talkin' that you want that UFO house.

"If it was me, I'd keep lookin'. Listen—you tryin' to get a new start and get your life under control. You got a habit of findin' dead people, and the live people in your life ain't all that normal, present company excepted. Now you want to buy a house that's got a nut in a tree and prob'ly has the ghost of that drowned kid hangin' around."

"I like my friends," I answered hotly. "And as for finding dead people, well, that's not my fault."

My cell phone rang, and I answered after recognizing my office number on the screen.

"What's up?"

"Whoa. You sound a little tense," responded Beth, who wasn't sounding light and bright herself.

"Sorry. I've been looking at houses. It's not as much fun as I thought it would be."

"I hear that. Dale and I"—Dale is Beth's husband—"must've looked at twenty houses before we found one we wanted. I couldn't believe what pigs some people were and what lousy taste others had. And the real-estate agents—don't get me started on them. Pushy doesn't begin to describe them. We had one that—"

"Were you calling about business?" I interrupted. I didn't need anyone to enlighten me about real-estate agents.

"Not exactly. I called to let you know that your mother is here."

I don't remember what happened next, although Tuwanda told me later that I turned white, dropped the phone, put my head on the table, and repeatedly moaned, "Why?"

She helped me to her car and got me home. After a couple of glasses of wine, my vocabulary expanded.

"This is terrible."

"What's terrible? You ain't said nothin' 'cept 'why' since you got off the phone with Beth. What's goin' on with you?"

"My mother is at my office."

I'd told Tuwanda before that my mother and I weren't close, but I'd never gotten into the specifics.

"She probably just wants to see her little girl. Come on. I'll drive you over."

"No!" I screamed.

Tuwanda started, and then her eyes narrowed. "You don' want me goin' with 'cuz I embarrass you."

"Absolutely not. I'm embarrassed by my *mother*. You have no idea."

I started shaking and had to put my glass down to keep from spilling wine.

"It can't be that bad," said Tuwanda. "We all got a family member or two that we like to think ain't genetically related. I told you about my mom. When she got drunk, she thought she was a geisha and powdered herself with flour, and she got drunk pretty much every day. Plus, I had an uncle who was on *World's Dumbest Criminals*. Twice. First time, he tried to rob a pet store an' ended up with a rottweiler attached to his butt. He's from my dad's side of the family, and they are determined to do dumb things. So as soon as my uncle got out of jail, he tried to rob a jewelry store. He triggered a silent alarm, and when the police showed up, he took off runnin' and hid in a buildin' down the street. The problem was the buildin' he was hidin' in was a police station."

I remained mutely abject. Tuwanda's family issues were small potatoes compared to mine.

She tsk-tsked. "You gotta tell me what the problem is. I can't help unless I know what's goin' on between you and your mom."

I wanted to confide in Tuwanda. I couldn't think of how to do it, though, partly because the situation was so complex, but mostly because after years of walling up memories and emotions, my ability to feel, much less share, feelings was severely impaired.

I once heard that our emotions influence how we experience life. If that's the case, my perceptions lack emotional input and are therefore incomplete, especially when it comes to my mother. My reaction to her was to shut down.

"If you can't tell me, maybe you should think about talkin' to a psychologist or psychiatrist. This reaction you havin' to a visit from your mom ain't normal. I'm not sayin' you need to go all lovey-dovey on her ass, but you afraid to even see her."

That last part snapped me out of it. "I'm not *afraid*. I would describe it more along the lines of a heightened sense of self-protection."

"I'll go with you. Nothin' can happen to you if I'm there."

"You don't know what she's like," I moaned. "She seems so nice, and you think you're having a wonderful conversation, but then suddenly, your self-esteem plummets, and you're paralyzed by depression. I don't know how she does it."

"I can use my special trainin' to observe an' throw some light on the situation."

Tuwanda had taken a psychology course at the community college last year.

"Then you'll have to talk to her yourself, because I'm not going," I said, stubbornly crossing my arms.

"Fine. I'll just go over to your office and explain that you ain't able to meet with her."

"No, you don't need to do that. I'll call Beth and ask her to explain that I don't have time for a visit right now."

"Beth knows damn well you have time, an' Beth don't lie."

Tuwanda was correct. Beth controls the allotment of my time. If nothing is written on Beth's calendar, then I'm not doing anything. She would know I could work in a visit with my mom, and since Beth is a strong Baptist for whom lying is a one-way ticket to hell, so would my mom.

I reconsidered Tuwanda's offer. "Do you promise to only tell her that I'm busy and nothing else?"

"Well, I don't know. What if she asks me somethin' simple, like how you're doin'. It'd be impolite not to answer."

"Walk away," I said. "Say nothing. Do not give her an opening."

"What if she asks how *I'm* doin'?"

"Run away."

Tuwanda rolled her eyes. "Now I'm curious as hell to meet her. Ain't no way a little old lady—what is she, in her seventies?—can be that evil."

"She's seventy-eight. And if you won't take my advice, I can't help you."

Tuwanda did another eye roll. She headed for the front door, grabbing her purse along the way. "You want me to call you after I talk to your mother?"

"Only if things go well." I was too emotionally frail for bad news.

"You gonna at least tell me her name? I can't go on callin' her Kate's mom."

"Mrs. Eleanor Williams. Do not under any circumstances call her Elly. In fact, the best thing to do is stick with Mrs. Williams. I do."

"I don't care how this ends up—you gonna get help," Tuwanda muttered as she exited.

I poured another glass of wine and, needing a distraction, sat in front of my computer to do a background check on the UFO house and the surrounding area.

I searched *Arcadia* first and skimmed through pages of chamber-of-commerce hype on the benefits of the neighborhood. A search of newspaper articles likewise reflected a closely knit community with A-rated schools, including a high school with a top-notch football team. Then I found an article about a backyard pool drowning about a year ago. The home's address was not given, but most of the facts fit, except that I had envisioned a toddler drowning, the result of an open gate and briefly unattended child. Although no less tragic, the victim in this case had been the homeowner's sixteen-year-old daughter. She had drowned during a pool party attended by kids from her school. The article did not say but implied that drugs and alcohol had been contributing factors. A picture of the girl, identified as Tiffany Jacobs, showed a beautiful young woman with long dark hair and eyes like those of Julia Roberts.

I switched to a less-devastating subject and googled *Phoenix UFO*. I came up with hundreds of search results. I'd had no idea the UFO community was so large. The incidents in Phoenix and northeast Arizona were the centerpieces of many of the articles. Apparently, if extraterrestrials existed, Arizona was the preferred landing site. Maybe they liked to golf. Or maybe they thought the Arizona population was primitive and preferred to start with a less-complex life-form. I could see how they could get the latter impression, based on the results of the last statewide elections.

The incident in 1997 was well documented, complete with pictures of the UFO, which indeed looked UFOish. To date, no human cause for the lights—at least no human cause acceptable to Arizonians—had been given by the US chief of staff.

The articles I read mentioned nothing about an abduction in the Phoenix lights incident, so either Nelsen hadn't reported it, or he had and his story had been dismissed as lacking credibility. The third option—that he'd made it up or imagined it—was the most likely, but I didn't like to think that about Nelsen. He seemed as normal as I. (Being odd does not mean you're abnormal.)

I next searched for other real-estate listings in the Arcadia and Encanto areas but found nothing that appealed to me as much as the UFO house. To be honest, though, I was going out of my way to find things wrong with the other homes. I was building a case for the UFO house despite its drawbacks.

I had been at my Internet research for a little more than two hours, when the phone rang. I picked up a millisecond before the call went to voice mail.

"Eleanor is wonderful!" enthused Tuwanda. "I jus' had coffee with her, and I don't get what you talkin' about. The woman's a saint."

I'd heard similar things from many people and was not impressed. "Did you explain that I wouldn't be able to get together with her?"

"I did, and you could tell she was hurt, but she was so nice about it. She said she knew you was a busy, important person, and she understood."

"You didn't tell her where I live, did you?"

"What's wrong with you, Kate? You got a great mom, and listen to you."

I groaned. The last thing I wanted was for my mother to come between Tuwanda and me. "How about we meet for coffee tomorrow? And I'll try to explain."

"Okay by me."

We agreed on a time and place and signed off.

Unless my mother had radically changed, I wouldn't need to give Tuwanda much of an explanation.

CHAPTER 4

We didn't meet for coffee after all. Tuwanda called the next morning while I was in the shower and left a message saying she was feeling blue and needed to take some private time.

It was not as if I hadn't warned her.

I knew from experience, though, that pulling away from friends after they've experienced one of my mom's neutron bombs was not a good idea. Depression worsens when the only voices you hear are the one inside your head and my mother's.

I called my office, told Beth I would be in late, and asked her to let me know if my mother showed up again, in which event I would not come in at all. Then I got dressed and headed for Tuwanda's house with Ralph in tow, thinking that after I revived Tuwanda, I would take Ralph for a walk in Arcadia to see how he liked the neighborhood.

I was hopeful my session with Tuwanda would be short. Two hours of exposure to my mother had to be easier to undo than the forty years I've had to deal with her.

I knocked with increasing tempo and intensity until my knuckles were red and painful. When Tuwanda finally answered the door, I could tell she was in a bad way.

Tuwanda is usually immaculately dressed regardless of the hour of day, but today she wore baggy gray sweatpants and a stained yellow sweatshirt with *Phoenix Shooting Club* printed on it. Her face bore the flat expression of the deeply depressed.

I didn't say anything but led her to the couch and headed to the kitchen to make coffee. Ralph, understanding the seriousness of the situation in the intuitive way dogs do, lay on the floor next to her and fell asleep.

When I returned shortly with two cups of steaming coffee, Tuwanda had slumped sideways, and her head was buried in a pillow.

I placed the coffee on a side table, pulled her into an upright position, and then handed her a cup before she could slide down again.

"Drink your coffee!" I ordered.

"I was thinkin' of somethin' along the lines of crack cocaine might be more helpful," she said in a monotone. She dutifully took a sip of coffee, though.

Tuwanda is extremely antidrug, having lost family members to addiction, and I've never heard her even joke about the subject.

A few sips later, she showed signs of life. Thank God for caffeine. (Some drugs are okay.)

"Do you want to tell me about it?" I asked softly.

"Ain't nothin' to tell. I'm jus' a failure. I ain't lived up to my potential. Hell, I ain't even lived up to Walter's potential."

Her teacup poodle, Walter, upon hearing his name, trotted in from the bedroom and jumped up onto her lap. She barely noticed him.

"What did you and my mother talk about?"

She smiled sadly. "Your mom is a nice lady. I enjoyed talkin' to her. She so upbeat, an' she knows all these important people an' stuff."

"Tell me exactly what she said."

"She went on and on about how beautiful I am an' about what great things I could do, an' she tol' me about this friend of hers jus' like me who's a senator now."

"Okay. Now, let me translate. She said you're pretty, but you haven't done a damn thing with your life, while other people like you are making a difference. By the way, did she happen to mention the name of her friend in the Senate?"

"Jus' a last name—Olson."

"FYI, Lester Olson is a seventy-four-year-old white guy who, after watching his last press conference, I'm convinced has Alzheimer's. My mother shook his hand and said hello thirty years ago when he was first running for office. Although she hasn't talked to him since, she still refers to him as her 'dear friend Senator Olson.' Plus, according to my mother, everyone has great potential, but no one lives up to it."

Tuwanda stared into her coffee contemplatively. "She always been like that?"

I nodded. "I got my first A on a spelling test in fourth grade, and when I showed it to her, she said, 'That's wonderful! When I was growing up, there was a girl in my class who was so smart she went to college at age ten! You could be like her.' But of course I couldn't, and I wasn't. I was a failure at ten."

"I understan' all that, an' I get why I feel the way I do now," said Tuwanda. "But if you know she hittin' them buttons, you can take a step back an' not let her get to you. She still your mom, an' she gettin' old. She ain't gonna be around much longer."

There is another reason I avoid my mother—and my sister as well—but I prefer to keep it buried. I could not, even then, think about it, much less discuss it. The shame, sadness, and alienation triggered by the slightest brush with certain memories were too much to handle.

I changed the subject, explaining my plan to take Ralph for a tour of Arcadia to determine his comfort level with the neighborhood.

"That's cheatin'. Ralph loves any place with lots of grass he can poop on, an' Arcadia's irrigated. It's the greenest place in town."

I invited Tuwanda and Walter to come with us, and Tuwanda accepted the offer. Walter's alacrity for the idea was a given. Thirty minutes later, Tuwanda was showered and dressed in a pink cotton tracksuit with tennis shoes that had cost more than my monthly mortgage. Walter was dressed in a matching tracksuit, except as a concession to his masculinity, his was blue.

The weather was unusually pleasant for September, with the mercury hovering around eighty degrees. This is sweater weather for Phoenicians.

I parked just inside the entrance to the subdivision in which the UFO house was located. Ralph was thrilled and tugged at his leash, stopping every few feet to sniff grass, rocks, entry monuments, mailboxes—whatever had an odor. Walter, who was off his leash, followed Tuwanda sedately, disdainful of Ralph's sniffing.

Ralph and I once attended a training session in an attempt to correct our behavioral issues. Ralph thought he was the alpha dog, and I had no problem with that. However, according to the trainer—a humorless man who wore GI khakis and yelled like a drill sergeant—*I* was supposed to be the alpha dog. Both Ralph and I were pronounced untrainable and sent home.

An odd thing happened when we were within sight of the UFO house. Ralph's ears perked up, he lost all interest in sniffing, and he made a beeline for the house.

"What'd you do—bury some meat in the front yard?" Tuwanda asked suspiciously between huffs and puffs as we tried to keep up with Ralph.

When we got to the house, Ralph stopped and flopped down in the front yard.

I was impressed. "Did you see that?" I asked excitedly.

"I'm here, ain't I? Did you train him to do that?"

I didn't bother to answer. Tuwanda knew Ralph had flunked dog school.

I looked at my watch. It was already noon. "Do you think Nelsen is here?"

"Prob'ly. His shift ain't over yet."

Since the house was empty, I saw no problem going into the backyard to say hi.

Tuwanda agreed to stay with the dogs while I went to find Nelsen.

He was in the tree, just as he'd said he would be, so I knew him to be a man of his word. I greeted him and climbed up to the branch I'd perched on the day before.

Nelsen was not in a chatty mood, however. He seemed sad and distracted. I wondered if the futility of his UFO watch was beginning to dawn on him.

I was about to give up on a conversation, when I heard voices coming from the house. I froze and watched apprehensively as Jane, followed by a couple who looked to be in their late thirties, emerged from the house. My first instinct was to blame Tuwanda for not warning me, but then I remembered I'd left my cell phone in the car. If she had tried to warn me by yelling, she would have given away my position.

Jane adroitly avoided the tree as she rolled out a sales spiel nearly identical to the one she had given to me the day before.

The couple didn't appear interested, however, and looked around the yard as if looking for something—or someone.

Jane's glib verbosity devolved into spurts of incoherent babbling as she executed fencing horse maneuvers to keep the man and woman away from the tree and its usual inhabitant.

Moving at sloth-like speed to avoid detection, I climbed to a higher limb, where the Aleppo's denser branches afforded me more protection. Nelsen did not move but watched the couple, who had turned their faces toward the tree and were staring in our direction with rigid concentration.

The man looked familiar, although I couldn't place him. His blond hair was brushed back off a high forehead, and although I was fairly sure he hadn't spotted us yet, his piercing blue eyes gave the uncomfortable impression of having X-ray capabilities.

The woman, who had matching blonde hair, gasped and grabbed the man's arm. With a shaking finger, she pointed at Nelsen.

Jane's shoulders slumped when she realized the jig was up.

The man approached the tree and stared into its limbs in much the same way I had the day before. Unlike me, he made no move to climb up.

"Dad!" he called out.

"Shit," muttered Nelsen.

"Dad! Dammit, get down here."

Nelsen said nothing in response. After a heavy silence, the blond man tried again.

"Don't make me come up there, Dad."

Yes. Please don't make him do that, I thought. I looked pleadingly at Nelsen, hoping to convey my feelings about the matter. Since Nelsen was looking fixedly at the blond man, my attempt at telepathic communication failed.

Despite my precarious position—both literally and figuratively—part of me was fascinated by the unfolding drama. Now that the blond man had pointed out the relationship, I could see the similarities between father and son. I could also see similarities between Nelsen and the blonde woman—his daughter perhaps?

The blond man moved closer to the tree and placed a Louis Vuitton-loafer-encased foot on its lowest branch.

"Go away," said Nelsen calmly, as if he were shooing a fly.

The blond man hesitated and then withdrew his foot from the branch.

"We want to help you, Dad." The blond man's voice had acquired a wheedling tone.

Nelsen snorted. "Run out of money again, did you?"

"Stop it, Dad," said the blonde woman. "This has gone on long enough. You have two grandchildren you've never met."

"And I suppose they've been brought up to believe their ole granddad is a head case. I think they feel just fine about not knowing me."

"That's not fair," said the blonde woman. "How can you say that? Please, Dad. You need to let us take you home."

Another long pause ensued before Nelsen spoke. "Tell you what—give me twenty-four hours to think about it. Come back here tomorrow, and I'll tell you my decision."

"There's no decision to make," said the blond man. "You are coming with us."

"No!" shouted Nelsen so loudly that I was startled and had to grab another branch to steady myself. "You have no right to order me around. I am still your father, young man. Now, leave so the nice lady can get on with her business."

Son and daughter looked at Jane, whom everyone had forgotten. "Thank you, sir," she said timidly. "I appreciate that. I have several showings—"

"Not you—the lady up here."

Everyone on the ground moved closer to the tree and looked up. Jane caught sight of me first.

"Hi, Jane," I said, giving her an anemic wave.

"Kate? Is that you?"

"Yes. I stopped by to take another look at the house." My explanation would have been easier to sell if I weren't sitting in a tree.

I caught a predatory glint in Jane's eyes. She was back on home turf. "Are you interested in making an offer?"

I didn't want to explain in front of the others that I'd gone there to reassure myself about Nelsen's future intentions. When I didn't answer right away, Jane said, "This couple is interested in buying this property, and several other prospective buyers are interested as well."

"Actually," said Nelsen's son, "we came to find my father. We contacted Jane because that was the only way to get in, short of trespassing."

"Like I said, there are several others interested in this house," Jane continued gamely.

"Well, I will certainly give it serious consideration," I said.

"You can come in with a lowball offer if you want. What would it hurt?"

Jane likely would have continued with the sales pressure, but Nelsen's son cleared his throat impatiently, and his sister's nonstop sighing had become distracting.

Jane relented and, after placing another sales brochure under the tree, left with Nelsen's kids.

"What was that about, Nelsen?"

"They're my kids. I knew it was a matter of time before they came here. They've been trying to commit me to a nuthouse on and off since I saw the aliens. They come after me whenever they need money," said Nelsen, answering my unspoken question but raising another.

Nelsen did not strike me as a wealthy man. Was this another delusion?

"Where do you sleep at night?" I asked softly.

"A place called the Sacred Bleeding Heart Shelter. I have a house, but I don't go there anymore."

I knew the shelter well. My "son" Larry slept on the shelter's roof. (Larry, a homeless man who thinks I'm his mother—it's a long story—is claustrophobic.)

"Are you married?"

"I'm not sure. My wife moved to San Diego with the pool man years ago."

Pools seemed to bring bad luck in this neighborhood.

"And she hasn't tried to get hold of you?"

"I'm not an easy man to get hold of. No phones or computers," he said, sweeping his arm around his perch.

"So what are you going to do? Your children seemed determined to bring you home."

"I'm not worried. I'll ignore them, and after a while, they'll go away. They don't stick with anything that's too much trouble."

Great, I thought. Nelsen *and* his family would be in the backyard until his kids got tired and left Nelsen to himself.

"How long does it usually take them to, er, go away?"

"Last time, they hung around for a week. Depends on how much they need the money."

"Aren't you afraid they'll file an action for involuntary commitment?"

"You're an attorney, right?"

I looked down and nodded. The looking down part is conditioning—admitting you're an attorney in most circles is like admitting you kick puppies.

"Afraid I've got a claim for adverse possession, are you?"

A sigh escaped from my mouth. "Look, Nelsen, I really like this house. I'm trying to figure out if I can make it work with you being in the tree four hours a day."

"I'm no Peeping Tom, so don't worry about me tryin' to look at anything you're doing. I only look at the sky."

"You gonna be up there much longer?" called Tuwanda. I had been so absorbed in my conversation with Nelsen that I hadn't noticed her approach, and now she was at the foot of the tree with Walter and Ralph. All three were looking up.

"Those your dogs?" asked Nelsen.

"Just the big one."

Ralph, sensing he was being talked about, frenetically wagged his tail.

"He seems friendly enough."

"He is. His worth as a guard dog is limited, though. Shedding is the only hazard he presents to a burglar."

Tuwanda introduced herself and exchanged pleasantries with Nelsen, who could not take his eyes off her and was obviously smitten.

Tuwanda insisted that I come down so that we could get some lunch. I asked Nelsen if he wanted us to bring anything back for him, but he said he was fine.

Once we were in the car with Walter and Ralph lying in an exhausted heap in the backseat, I told Tuwanda what had happened and gave her a rundown of my conversation with Nelsen.

"It's interestin' that he's stayin' at the Bleeding Heart Shelter. You think Larry knows him?"

"The shelter isn't that big. I'm sure Larry's at least seen him and maybe even talked to him. Whether Larry remembers it is a separate issue."

"You gonna ask Larry 'bout him?"

"I think I might—maybe just a phone call." However, with only one phone at the shelter, phone calls to Larry were not easy. "There's something that doesn't make sense about Nelsen's situation."

"Everythin' don't make sense about Nelsen's situation."

"I mean that except for the UFO and tree-sitting thing, Nelsen is coherent and seems normal. Also, he appears to have some money—at least enough to interest his kids. Money management takes a sharp mind, and I got the impression he was handling his own affairs."

My brain cells in charge of curiosity had taken over and were holding the practical brain cells hostage, threatening them with atrophy unless the curious cells got what they wanted.

After lunch, I dropped off Tuwanda, Walter, and Ralph (Tuwanda had invited Ralph for a sleepover) and, after getting the all clear from Beth (my mother was not around), headed to my office to get some work done.

Beth, MJ, and Sam looked at me questioningly when I walked in, but I didn't enlighten them as to the reason for my mother-avoidance tactics. Beth seemed kind of down, though, so I think maybe she was catching on to at least part of the problem.

I love Beth, but I neither had the time nor was in the mood to hold another therapy session.

I walked over to her, gave her a hug, and then placed my hands on her shoulders. Looking into her eyes, I said, "You are a worthwhile person who has made a difference in the lives of everyone you know."

I gave her shoulders a squeeze and headed for my office.

I froze in the doorway when I caught sight of the pink sheet of paper lying on top of my desk. The smell of my mother's perfume wafted across the room. She had worn the same scent for fifty years and liberally sprayed every piece of correspondence with it—even bill payments. A whiff of the stuff in a crowd is enough to trigger a mild panic attack in me.

I lifted the paper by a corner as if it were a ticking bomb and shoved it into the drawer of my credenza. Then I grabbed a can of Febreze off the bathroom shelf and sprayed the room.

When I was sure I had obliterated the perfume smell, I sat behind my desk and tried to review a motion to dismiss I was arguing the next day in front of Judge Weiner. My mind had different ideas. First, it wandered to the subject of my mother. After I successfully redirected it, it drifted off again, this time to the UFO house, Nelsen, and his children.

Finally giving in to distraction, I turned to my computer and googled Nelsen Nelsen. I narrowed the search to the Phoenix area after getting thousands of hits. Apparently, Nelsen Nelsen is a common name, especially in the Midwest.

Even after restricting the search to Phoenix, I had a fair number of hits. I eliminated those with Facebook accounts, since I doubted my Nelsen published on vanity sites—or any site, for that matter. It's hard to climb a tree with a laptop.

I found an article on a site called Beam Me Up that described the 1997 UFO sighting in great detail, with several firsthand accounts of witnesses to the event. One of those witnesses was identified as "Mr. Nelsen Nelsen, owner-operator of a local wholesale bakery." According to Nelsen, he'd climbed a nearby tree—and I knew which tree—to get a better look at the UFO, when a beam of light hit him and he was transported into a triangular spaceship. He was met by a group of what he believed were four aliens, although as he explained, "it could have been one alien with four heads and bodies." They were wearing space suits, so he couldn't get a good look at them, but one of them removed its glove to touch him, and he noticed its skin was gelatinous and clear.

He said that overall, they were polite and seemed to want only to look at him. Things were going well until an air force jet flew by and spooked the aliens, who then sent him back to the tree.

Nelsen was the only witness the reporter talked to who was abducted, but several other witnesses attested to seeing the UFO, including then-governor Fyfe Symington and the county supervisor, Rose Wilcox.

I checked the archives of the *Republic*, the local newspaper, which went back as far as 1995 online. The 1997 UFO sightings had been big news for quite some time, as Wilcox had continued to push the feds for an explanation of the mysterious lights in the sky. By 1999, the articles tapered off, but not until the national media had had a mountain of fun at Arizona's expense.

The only other mention of Nelsen's name was an announcement in September 1995 about the opening of a new wholesale bakery operation in South Phoenix.

There was a light tap at the door, and Sam entered. As usual, he was immaculately dressed in a Brioni suit nicely set off by a white shirt, a striped tie, and strappy red sandals with four-inch heels. (Sam has yet to wear heels outside the office or in the presence of clients but feels comfortable enough around us to wear his beloved Jimmy Choos.)

He sat across the desk from me without asking. (We do not stand on ceremony in my office—or even, for that matter, require especially good manners.)

"Things are getting weird around here again," he said, starting without preface.

Since the weirdness bar in my office is set high, this was bad news.

"Lily?" I asked.

Lily is a little girl who died in the crawl space beneath our building more than fifty years ago. Lily's spirit gets blamed for most of the odd occurrences in our office.

"Maybe. That could explain how all the case files were rearranged."

"Rearranged? As in no longer in alphabetical order?"

"Rearranged as in every piece of paper is not where it should be. It's as if someone emptied all the files and then shuffled them like cards."

This news was disturbing but not catastrophic, since we maintain computer file copies as well.

"Anything else?" I asked.

"Your mother—"

I clutched the arms of my chair and looked around wildly for an escape route.

"She's not here, is she?"

"No. She hasn't been in yet today. But yesterday she was here most of the day. She said she didn't want to bother anyone, so she turned a chair in the reception area to face a wall and sat there all day except for bathroom breaks. For someone who didn't want to bother anyone, she sure was. Thank God Tuwanda came and took her out for coffee. I was tired of explaining the situation to every client who walked in."

"How did you explain her?"

"I told them she hadn't paid her bill, so she was in time out."

"Good save."

"Beth gave her a ride to her hotel at the end of the day," he continued. "Now Beth is convinced she's wasted her life."

My heart went out to her.

"Did she get to you and MJ yet?"

"I was busy all afternoon, and no one can get to MJ. She's impervious to all forms of criticism—even constructive criticism."

If anyone knew, Sam would.

"If your mother comes in again, you need to talk to her, Kate."

"Nothing I have said to my mother in forty years has made any impact on her behavior. She's here for her own reasons. I can guarantee you it has nothing to do with me. When she's accomplished whatever it is she came to do, she will leave. Until then, I will continue to survive as I have in the past—I will avoid her."

"You've avoided your mother your entire life? Were you raised by wolves?"

"No. As a child, I was an expert at dissociation. My body may have been in the room, but my mind was far away."

"Seriously?"

I nodded.

"Kate, everyone's parents drive them crazy. My mother always sets me up with her friends' daughters, and she knows damn well I'm gay. She figures it's a phase and I just haven't met the right woman yet."

I shrugged. There was more, but the past is the past, and I couldn't change it, so why talk about it?

A familiar sense of hopelessness overwhelmed me.

"Your father must have balanced out things; otherwise, you'd be a complete fruitcake," commented Sam.

My smile did not reach my eyes.

Sam threw up his hands dramatically. "Fine. Don't divulge. What do you want us to do if she comes in again?"

I gave his question some thought. My mother was sharp. The plan had to be subtle and seamless.

"Tell Beth to buzz me on the intercom three times. I will leave through the window. Does my mother know what kind of car I drive?"

"I never told her, but I'll check with MJ and Beth."

"Let me know what they say. If she knows, you'll have to move my car. Park it near the children's park on Sixth Street," I said, handing him my keys.

"Should I go home and change into black ninja clothes, or am I okay to do this as is?"

"You've got a ninja costume?"

"Of course. Dean and I like to dress—"

Dean is Sam's latest boyfriend.

"I really should get back to work," I interrupted. "Is there anything else I should know about? I mean business stuff?"

"That's it for now. But the day isn't over." Sam stood and saluted. "I will stay in contact, sir."

He performed a perfect one-point pivot and left. Sam had the balance of a runway model.

I took another shot at reviewing the next day's court case, but my heart and mind still weren't in it. I printed out copies of the articles mentioning Nelsen, and I told Beth that I was leaving and she was therefore relieved from her warning-buzzer duties. Then I retrieved my car keys from Sam and headed for South Phoenix. My half-formed plan was to locate Nelsen's bakery, and then I didn't know.

The *Republic* article hadn't mentioned the bakery's street address, but in that part of town, most of the businesses are located on Broadway or Southern.

I took freeway 51 to I-10 and exited at Broadway and Forty-Fourth Street, thinking I would drive the stretch from Forty-Fourth to Twentieth and then head south to Southern and head east back to Forty-Fourth.

As I drove west along Broadway, the modern light-industrial complexes and business offices gave way first to bars, fast-food restaurants, and Circle Ks and then to hole-in-the-wall restaurants and ma-and-pa grocery stores separated from each other by long stretches of bladed lots with weathered For Sale signs. No one was buying property down there in the bad economy. Even in a good economy, businesses didn't locate in South Phoenix absent heavy city subsidies.

A block back from the main drag, small houses stood so close together that they almost touched. Although relatively new homes, courtesy of the city's sporadic low-cost housing efforts, were interspersed throughout the area, the structures were, for the most part, bungalows hastily erected in the fifties to accommodate Phoenix's burgeoning post-World War II population. Although some showed pride of ownership, most were dilapidated and had bare-dirt, junk-filled yards crisscrossed with utility wires and clotheslines. The ambiance was one of unremitting poverty.

A well-tended building stood out, however. A sign identified it as the Pioneer Presbyterian Church. I pulled into an adjacent lot and parked.

Children of various ages played in a dusty playground behind the church. Behind the playground was a community garden populated by people hard at work weeding, hoeing, and cleaning out irrigation ditches.

After asking directions from several polite but wary people, I located the church office. A woman whose beauty rivaled Tuwanda's greeted me and asked if she could help me with anything. A plastic name tag identified her as Rose.

I introduced myself, explained that I was a local attorney, and gave her my business card. Then I got down to business. "I'm looking for a wholesale-bakery operation. It's supposed to be in this area, but so far, I haven't had any luck finding it."

"You must mean Nelsen's bakery," she said promptly.

"Yes! That's exactly what I mean."

The eponymous bakery had to be the one I was looking for.

"Are you a prospective buyer? That building's been empty since the late nineties. The people in this community would love to see it operating again. A lot of jobs were lost when it shut down."

"Do you know why it shut down?"

"Uh-uh. It's a real pity, though. I remember how the whole neighborhood used to smell like baking bread. I loved that. Now it smells like—well, it smells like nothing."

"The bakery couldn't have been operating that long. I read somewhere it opened in 1995."

"That was the *new* facility. The old one was built in 1967. Mr. Nelsen came down here to do business when no one else would after the riots in 1964. My dad used to work for him.

"I'm just guessing, but maybe what happened was that the new equipment cost too much and the business couldn't make it. But one day, there was a Closed sign on the door—and not a word about it from Nelsen."

"And it's stood there empty more than ten years now?"

"I don't know that I'd say empty—" She seemed to catch herself.

"How far is it from here?" I asked.

She motioned for me to follow her outside. We walked to the edge of the playground, and she pointed across an empty field to a three-story brick structure. Every window was broken, and the yard was littered with old tires, rusted bits of machinery, and trash. The building looked foreboding even in daylight.

I thanked Rose and headed to my car. I was reaching for the door handle, when I felt a sharp pain on the back of my head.

"Sorry!" yelled a little boy standing behind the chain-link fence surrounding the playground. "Could you get that?"

I looked around and saw a worn basketball bouncing toward the road, on its way to cause more havoc. I grabbed it before it rolled into traffic and threw it back over the fence.

"What you doin' here talkin' to Miss Rose?" he asked.

I judged his age to be around eight or nine.

"Getting directions to that building over there," I said, pointing at the bakery.

"My grandma says bad things go on there, and I can't go nowhere near it. I guess your grandma don't care about that stuff."

"Jevon!" called a masculine voice. "Don't you be botherin' that lady."

I waved at the speaker, a tall black man wearing work clothes and carrying a load of gardening tools.

He nodded to me and then ordered Jevon to help carry "some of this stuff."

When I pulled out of the parking lot, the man was heading toward the garden with the little boy following closely behind, dragging a rake twice his size.

I drove south to the next cross street and turned left toward the bakery. I had no intention of getting out of my car, much less going in the building. I was curious only as to whether it existed, and now I knew that it did and that the timing of the plant closing roughly corresponded with Nelsen's UFO sighting and abduction. I only planned to take a picture of the bakery with my cell phone and then leave.

As I drew closer, I could see that the broken windows were covered with chicken wire. The front of the building, perhaps because it faced away from the busy traffic on Broadway, was covered with graffiti. The usual gang signs were there, but so were amazing examples of street art—smiling children, Martin Luther King and Malcolm X, and a garden resembling the one behind the church.

I pulled to the side of the road and parked, leaving my motor running. I was admiring the artwork, when out of the corner of my eye, I noticed movement behind a third-story window. I focused on the window and saw it again. And again. And again. I tried to dismiss it as no more than a hanging bit of curtain or rope moving rhythmically in the wind. The problem was that there was no wind.

The swinging object slowed to stasis, and I got a better look at it. It was a person—or, more precisely, the head of a person, because that was all I could see through the window. From the angle of the head, I guessed the person was dead.

I wasn't looking forward to the inevitable comments about "Kate finding another one," but my sense of shock and duty prevailed, and I made the 911 call.

I gave my name and coordinates and described the situation. After the operator contacted dispatch, she got back on the line.

"Hey, Kate. It's Lorraine."

"Hi, Lorraine," I answered.

"We were just talkin' about you at lunch today," she continued, either not picking up on my lack of enthusiasm or choosing to ignore it. "We figured you were about due to call."

I sighed. "I don't know how to explain it, but it's wearing thin."

"That's okay. We think your calls are refreshin'. You just spit out the facts, real professional-like. It's better than most of what we get. I'm always sayin' things like, 'Sir, I cannot help you unless you stop screaming.'"

Oddly, her comment made me feel better even though it did nothing to solve the problem of why I see more bodies in a year than the coroner.

After I finished talking to Lorraine, I turned off my car's engine (and the air conditioner) and then tried the building's front door. I wrapped a plastic grocery bag around my hand first to preserve evidence, although suicide was more likely than murder in light of the circumstances. Most murderers don't favor hanging as a mode of execution, especially in a state where you can buy guns in a drugstore or at a gas station.

After determining that the door was locked, I scanned the windows for another point of entry. I spotted one on the first floor where the chicken wire had been rolled back. I went to the window and peered inside. Cool, urine-scented air wafted out. Once my eyes adjusted to the dark, I could see piles of litter consisting primarily of empty chip bags, plastic shopping bags, newspapers, and the occasional condom. Since the victim was clearly beyond the rescue stage, I decided not to risk entry.

I waited in my car until a patrol car pulled up behind me thirty minutes after I'd made the 911 call. Incidents in South Phoenix receive a lower priority than those in other parts of the city.

A police officer approached my car while his partner watched, his hand resting on top of his gun handle. The former was an older man, perhaps in his fifties, with tired eyes and a paunch. The latter looked as if he were barely out of high school. Thin with a pimpled face, he should have been picking up balls after basketball practice, not protecting the public.

I started to get out of my car but slid back into the seat when the older officer ordered me not to move and to keep both hands on the dash.

I wondered if they had my 911 call confused with someone else's.

The officer, whose name tag identified him as Jeff Bridges (really), asked for my name and address and then asked me for my driver's license, which I produced as he watched me warily with his hand on his gun to make sure I wasn't going for a weapon.

He finally got around to asking me why I had called in.

"Third-story window, fifth from the right," I answered. Pointing would have been easier, but he had not rescinded the hands-on-the-dashboard order.

Jeff and his partner looked up, and I could see their mouths move as they counted to five.

The sun was setting by this time, so the light was fading. The human head was barely visible through the dirty window.

Jeff asked the other officer, whom he addressed as Lonny, to get a flashlight. After a brief search of the patrol car's trunk, Lonny returned with a flashlight and handed it to Jeff.

Jeff flicked the switch and—nothing. He flicked it a few more times with the same result.

"Lonny, you were supposed to check the equipment this morning."

"I did. The battery must have died after I checked."

"Then if you checked everything, you made sure we had backup batteries. Go get 'em."

Lonny shrugged and said, "I didn't see no batteries in supply this morning. Besides, I didn't know we needed 'em."

Jeff looked at the window. "Then you'll have to go inside anyway and check things out."

"Without a flashlight?"

"I guess so."

"I have a little flashlight you can use," I offered, taking pity on Lonny.

"Thanks, miss. I'll take it," he said.

I took a penlight off my key chain and handed it to him. He looked disappointed.

"The front door is locked, but there's a window you can use to get in. I noticed it while I was waiting for you."

I could have watched a Friends *rerun and gotten my nails done before you got here*, I thought.

After asking and receiving permission, I got out of my car and led them to the window where the chicken wire had been pulled back.

Lonny started to protest, but Jeff interrupted him. "C'mon. I'll give you a leg up."

Jeff boosted Lonny through the window using what appeared to be unnecessary force. I heard Lonny's body hit the floor and the rustling of paper as he tried to stand.

"Gross," he said. He followed up this professional assessment with a string of expletives.

A few minutes later, Lonny shouted, "The door to the stairs is locked! I can't get up there."

"Deal with it," Jeff shot back.

Jeff was short on mentoring skills.

I heard thumping, separated by seconds of silence. I guessed Lonny was trying to kick in the door.

The thumping eventually stopped, and I heard the sharp report of a gun.

"Exigent circumstances," Jeff informed me.

The exigent circumstances disappeared about an hour ago, I thought.

Lonnie's voice floated down a few minutes later. "We've got the dead body of a male up here. Cause of death looks like hanging."

His tone changed with the latter pronouncement, and he sounded unsure and nervous.

Jeff noticed the difference too. "Anything else?" he called.

"It's not a local."

At first, I didn't get the meaning of Lonnie's cryptic remark, and I wondered if he had found some identification on the dead man that indicated he was an out-of-towner. Then a suspicious thought occurred to me.

"Is that code for 'He's white'?" I asked.

Jeff wasn't listening, though. He was on his phone, asking for backup and rattling off a series of crime codes I didn't recognize. After he hung up, he called to Lonny, telling him to stay put and not touch anything. He then paced between the street and the front of the building, muttering, "Damn, damn, damn, damn."

The next wave of law enforcement responded quickly. The dissonant chorus of sirens soon filled the air. In quick succession, another patrol car, an EMT truck, a fire-company ladder truck, and a sheriff's car pulled up in front of the building. Of these, the ladder truck was the most useful, as it provided a means for direct access to the third floor.

Officer Bridges told me to wait in my car until I was released. He took my keys despite my repeated assurances that I was not a flight risk. In his defense, I think he assumed anyone with a lick of sense would be a flight risk in this part of town.

It took them about a half hour to lower the body to the ground through the window. Before it was placed in the EMT truck, Officer Bridges motioned for me to come over.

Unzipping the body bag to reveal the corpse's face, he asked if I recognized him.

I did. I wished like heck that I didn't, but I did. It was Nelsen. Another officer, Officer Strait, one of the two who had come in the second patrol car, took my statement. We sat in the lighted interior of his car as I explained as much as I knew. Although Officer Strait looked up from his writing periodically, his face reflecting a mixture of doubt and surprise, he said nothing.

I didn't blame him for his reaction. The tree and the UFO angles were hard to swallow. You had to be there.

After I finished, Officer Bridges came over, returned my keys, and told me I could leave, adding that the police would likely want to speak to me again.

I slowly walked to my car, weighed down by shock and sadness. I had not known Nelsen that well, but he had seemed harmless and, in a way, rather sweet. I hadn't picked up on any suicidal tendencies, but maybe the visit of his son and daughter and the threat of involuntary commitment had triggered his decision to take his own life. I thought it odd he would choose to die in his abandoned bakery, since he seemed to have cut himself off from his past life, but again, I didn't know enough about him to understand his reasoning.

I was in my car with the key in the ignition, when a rap on the window startled me out of my sad musings. A face I did not recognize stared at me through the window.

I opened the door rather than lowering the window, figuring that with all the police around, there was a slim possibility of stranger danger. The man backed up as the door swung open, and then he stuck out his hand in greeting.

"George Booker," he said.

I shook his hand and introduced myself in return.

After a pause during which he appeared to be sizing me up, he said, "I am the pastor of the church you visited earlier today. You spoke to Rose, our church secretary. She said you're an attorney."

I nodded encouragingly, not sure where this conversation was going.

"We overheard when you identified the dead man."

When I looked at him questioningly, he pointed to a small group of people standing across the street—neighbors perhaps—who had come to see what was going on.

"Although none of us has seen him in a while, Mr. Nelsen is well regarded in this neighborhood, though some people think he abandoned our community when the bakery stopped operating. Since the business closed, this building has been used by junkies, homeless people, and teenagers hooking up. We complained to the city about it for years, but they didn't do anything. Not long ago, we took matters into our own hands and planned to clean it up ourselves and use it as a community center."

Reverend Booker admitted he had not talked to Nelsen recently, and I couldn't imagine Nelsen's children agreeing to such an arrangement, so I assumed the community-center plan had not been approved by the owner.

"That seems like a good idea," I offered, still not sure where this was going.

"I and many members of my congregation have been in that building at one time or another over the past few weeks, taking measurements, assessing damage—that kind of thing."

I was beginning to understand. "You're concerned the police will discover your prints all over a crime scene."

He nodded seriously. "Where there's a dead white man in a black community, the police make lots of accusations but do very little listening."

"The initial assessment is suicide. I don't think this is a crime scene," I said.

Pastor Booker looked toward the EMT van, where the body was being loaded. "God bless his soul," he said softly. "I wish I could have been here to stop him. Despair is no reason to die."

The man's sincerity moved me. Impulsively, I took a business card out of my purse and handed it to him. "Let me know if things change and you need help."

"I have to tell you we can't afford—"

"No charge."

My staff would have killed me if they'd heard what I said. I have a tendency to take on more pro bono work than is wise in operating a for-profit business. I can't seem to stop myself.

I will always be on the side of the underdog, and underdogs are usually broke.

As I drove away, I reasoned that the matter would likely be resolved as a suicide, so my services would not be needed. That being the case, I figured there was no reason to mention to my staff that I'd taken on another pro bono client.

I was wrong.

CHAPTER 5

It was dark by the time I left, and streetlights are few and far between once you get off the main drags in South Phoenix. I drove slowly through the neighborhood, guided by the faint light from the windows of small houses, through which I spotted residents peering out at the strange vehicle on their turf. The hum of swamp coolers fighting a losing battle against high temperatures drowned out other night noises.

A group of adolescents had collected at the Twenty-Fourth Street intersection. The mostly male members eyed me with an overt bravado that made me uncomfortable. As I turned north, a tall young man who, despite the heat, was wearing a black knit hat slapped the trunk as I passed by, as if to say, "Be on your way. You have no business here."

I called my office, and Sam picked up.

I got right to the point. "I found another one."

Sam did not need to ask what I was talking about. "Who? How? Where?"

I gave him an abbreviated version of what I had told Officer Strait.

"So you found the body of a man in South Phoenix who you'd met in a tree in Arcadia?"

"Pithy," I commented.

"A talent acquired through Twitter use. Kate, I don't want to be a doomsayer, but if Nelsen was murdered—and most of the people you find have been—the police may view you as a suspect."

"Why? Because he liked to sit in a tree in the backyard of a house I'm interested in buying? That's fairly attenuated."

"Stated differently, you just happened to be in South Phoenix in time to discover the body of a man whose presence ruined the otherwise perfect home you want to purchase. What the heck were you doing in that part of town? I've lived in Phoenix all my life, and I've been in that area one time—by mistake."

"Why don't you come down here more often?" I pressed.

"Because … well, you know why."

Yes, I did, and the fact that he couldn't say it told me he was ashamed to admit it. Sam prides himself on being open-minded and accepting of all people.

I took pity on him and added more detail as to why I had gone to South Phoenix. After I was finished, he said he would tell Beth and MJ what had happened, to save me the trouble.

"Don't say anything about the incident to my mother if she shows up," I warned.

"She has, and I won't."

I glanced at my watch. "It's after six. What is she doing there?"

"She decided the reception room looked dull and uninviting, so she's redecorating."

I groaned. I knew my mother's taste—pastel fabrics, ruffles, and paintings of little kids with big eyes.

I heard a voice in the background, and Sam excused himself for a second. I could not make out the conversation that followed, but a lot more than a second passed before he finally got back on the line.

"That was your mom. She's going to Joanne's to buy more fabric," he said.

Joanne's is a big-box store that sells fabric, sewing accessories, and every craft item imaginable. Somehow, I didn't think the makeover was going to stop with the reception area.

It looked as if mother was digging in. Something was going on.

I signed off with Sam and called a number I had not used in years—that of my sister, Paula.

My sister and mother are like two peas in a pod. They belong to the same clubs, enjoy the same hobbies, and share the same outlook on life, which generally consists of believing they are morally superior to everyone else. Both have the sensitivity of Edi Amin. If I stood in front of them with an ax in my head, their joint response would be along the lines of, "What a shame. But other people in the world have it so much worse. I have a friend who walked around with *two* axes in her head for a month without complaining. Where should we go to lunch?" Theirs is a deeply entrenched denial that filters out all facts that contradict their illusion of perfection.

After the fourth ring, Paula picked up. "Hello?" Her midwestern accent was all over the word.

"Hi, Paula. It's Kate."

"Kate, hi! I'm heading out to play bridge with some of the girls. Can I call you back?"

I'd like to think that if she called me after three years of silence, I would drop whatever I was doing to talk to her. That is not Paula's way, however.

"I only need a few seconds of your time." *Your precious bridge-playing time.* "As I'm sure you know, Mom is here. Do you know why?"

"No, but I'll bet the weather is wonderful. I'm sure she'll have a good time. Okay, gotta fly."

Click.

My mother and sister resort to false gaiety whenever something is wrong. My sister's omission of chatty oblique or overt references to her highly principled and productive life was also a dead giveaway that something was amiss.

There was no way around it. Either I talked to my mother and figured out how to deal with whatever was going on, or I moved and left no forwarding address.

I decided to put off talking to her until the next day. I'd had enough stress for one day. Confronting my mother on the same day I found another body was too much. I needed a couple of glasses of wine and a good night's sleep before confronting Mom. In the meantime, I had more-important things to do. Now that Nelsen was dead, it seemed even more important to find out more about him in order to make the pieces of the puzzle fit.

I called the communal phone at the Our Lady of the Bleeding Heart Shelter. A man answered after twelve rings, notified me that he was no longer accepting offers, and asked me to please stop calling. I asked to speak to Larry before he could hang up, and because I have a fatalistic streak, I asked what the offers were for.

"Marriage," he replied in an of-course tone.

I waited for the highly sought-out potential marriage partner to track down Larry, carrying on intermittent, wildly diverse conversations with residents who wandered by and picked up the dangling receiver out of curiosity. I was listening to a woman explain a conspiracy theory involving Wisconsin cheese and the health industry, when Larry broke in.

"Hi, Mom," he said cheerily.

This moniker made me grimace, but I didn't correct him. It wouldn't have done any good. "Hi yourself, Larry. How are things?"

Larry always took this sort of polite inquiry seriously and answered at length and in detail. When he finished, I explained the reason I was calling.

"Nelsen? Sure, I know Nelsen. He comes up on the roof sometimes to watch the stars with me. Of course, he's looking for UFOs, and I'm contemplating the effects of dark matter and dark energy on the configuration of a metauniverse. Still, he's good company."

"Did Nelsen ever talk to you about his personal life?"

"A bit. I know he has kids and that he doesn't like 'em much. Mostly, though, he goes on about his alien friends. I think he might have crush on one of 'em. He said he was going to change his will and leave everything to Xrtgam."

"Xrtgam?"

"That's what it sounded like to me. I didn't ask him about it, because I figured he didn't have much to leave, so it didn't matter.

"Why are we talking about Nelsen? Did something happen to him? No offense, Mom, but you got a talent for finding dead people, so it's a natural question."

I hated to be the bearer of bad news, but it was part of the body-discovering gig.

I told Larry about Nelsen.

Larry was so quiet that I wondered if he'd hung up. After a while, he said, "Suicide doesn't fit Nelsen's profile."

My first thought was that Larry had been watching too many *Criminal Minds* reruns. But then he clarified.

"Except for the part about not liking his kids, Nelsen was real positive about the future. He looked forward to seeing the aliens again. I got the feeling he thought he was close to being abducted again. He told me about the temperature in outer space and that he was stockpiling coats."

By this time, I had reached the underground garage of my condo building, and the phone signal was getting iffy. I signed off with Larry, promising to drop off a box of Twinkies, his favorite food, the next day.

My condo was quiet and lonely without Ralph. He was no doubt enjoying his sleepover with Walter, but under the circumstances, I needed some dog time. Stroking Ralph's thick fur always lowers my blood pressure, and his worshipful presence boosts my mood. His positive attributes outweigh the inconvenience of picking dog hairs off my clothes and out of the jelly jar.

I searched for Her as a substitute, but unlike Ralph, she has an independent streak, and when she doesn't want to be found, she is impossible to locate.

Bryan was at a fundraising dinner, so he couldn't serve as Ralph's stand-in either, and Mark was in Chicago at a personal-trainer convention.

My need for warm-blooded comfort was finally meliorated when, after I curled up on the on the couch with a glass of wine, Her crawled out from under a sofa cushion, jumped lightly onto my lap, and kneaded me with her feet. It felt like a mini-massage.

I tried watching television, but the stations I turned to either showed somber newscasters reporting the discovery of Nelsen's body or reruns of *CSI*, *NCIS*, or *Law & Order*.

Tuwanda, Macy, and Cal, having seen the news, all called to express their concern, but none of them conveyed surprise. Kate finding another body was unremarkable.

I dined on the single woman's special—a peanut-butter-and-jelly sandwich, an apple, and three glasses of white wine—and was getting ready for bed when the phone rang.

"Hi, Kate," bubbled Jane. "Whoa, you've had a full day."

She made it sound as if I'd been shopping and then played tennis instead of discovering the body of a man I knew and liked. Her superficial good cheer rivaled that of my mother and sister.

I was pondering whether superficiality had a genetic component, when Jane interrupted my train of thought.

"Kate? Are you there?"

"Uh, yes. Sorry. I got distracted by something. Do you, by chance, have any relatives in Minnesota?"

"What? What was that?"

"Nothing. What can I do for you, Jane?"

"Well, as you know, Mr. Nelsen passed on."

Yes, I discovered his body, you nit.

"It was his time. The cycle of life goes on."

The problem with her theory was that either Nelsen or someone else had jammed a stick in the spokes of Nelsen's cycle of life, and he'd died before his time.

I didn't say anything and let Jane squirm. There is nothing shallow people hate more than silence. The accompanying void invites invasive thoughts that destroy the pleasant buzz of lack of self-awareness.

"Anyway, I was thinking," she began unsteadily. "Have you reconsidered the Arcadia house in light of the changed circumstances?"

I couldn't believe her lack of taste and tact.

"I'll have to get back to you on that one, Jane. I'm still trying to recover from finding Nelsen's body swinging from the rafters in an abandoned building."

"I—oh, I see. Well then, we'll touch base tomorrow."

According to Jane, the recovery period for discovering a body is twenty-four hours, max.

I hung up on her.

I got little sleep that night between reliving the day's events and developing a rough outline of what I was going to say to my mother if and when I ran into her. At one point, my will wavered, and I considered handling the mother issue through written correspondence. Maybe I could find a card. Hallmark had cards for everything, and uncomfortable conversations always sound better when they rhyme.

By morning, I accepted that there was no way to avoid a face-to-face confrontation with Mrs. Williams. I had to make it clear that I could not countenance her interference in my business and personal life, and she needed to leave alone or leave.

At risk was losing the shaky confidence I'd established by living on my own. I knew the issues between my mother and I would never be resolved. The most I could hope for was polite distance.

I dreaded the mom talk and welcomed the temporary reprieve I got when Bryan called.

"Good morning, gorgeous. I'm sorry I didn't call you last night, but I didn't leave the dinner until midnight and figured you'd be asleep. It's not that I'm getting casual about your corpse discoveries. I just thought you wouldn't want to be woken up."

"That's okay," I said ruefully. "I wouldn't blame you if the novelty was wearing off. From my perspective, though, it never gets easier. This time, it was someone I knew—a harmless guy who just wanted to be abducted by aliens again."

There was a pause on Bryan's end of the line. "Come again?"

I sighed. "Never mind."

"Listen, Kate, part of the reason I'm calling is that I want to give you a heads up: the PD has decided Nelsen's suicide looks suspicious. You should expect a call from Detective

Ratchet regarding what is now classified as a possible homicide."

In response to my unasked question, he said, "Webber is on vacation."

Detective Webber has been assigned to so many of the cases in which I've been involved that I am convinced the police department has established a Dead People Discovered by Kate Williams Division, headed by Webber.

"Vacation?" I asked, not bothering to hide my surprise. "Webber never takes vacations."

"It's not exactly what I would call a vacation, but it's the closest he's come yet. He's a parent volunteer at his daughter's cheer camp in Flagstaff."

This revelation was like hearing that Arnold Schwarzenegger was playing Annie on Broadway.

"Those poor children," I murmured.

I dragged my mind away from the terrifying image of innocent young people being exposed to a bitingly sarcastic homicide cop.

"Why do the police suspect murder?"

"You'll have to ask Ratchet. I'm not at liberty to say."

I hated it when Bryan pulled the cop card on me.

"Thanks for the heads-up about very little," I groused.

"Kate, it's not my investigation. You know darn well that Ratchet will want to observe your reaction when he questions you."

"What? Do you think I had anything to do with—"

Bryan interrupted me in midsputter. "No, of course not. I have to be careful these days—follow the rules. You know that."

He was referring to his campaign for sheriff. In a conservative county, when you are running on a law-and-order ticket, the last thing you want is a legal scandal involving your bleeding-heart defense-attorney girlfriend. Bryan had already taken a risk by telling me about the turn in the investigation.

"I understand," I said. "By the way, any chance we can sneak in a dinner date this weekend?"

"Only if you want to go to the B'nai B'rith or the Italian-American dinner."

I groaned. "No thanks."

I couldn't wait until the election was over. It was destroying half my social life. I made a note to call Mark later—the other half of my social life—to see if he could go to dinner. He was due back from Chicago later in the day.

As soon as Bryan and I signed off, my cell phone started to ring.

"Miss Williams?" asked an official-sounding voice when I picked up.

"*Ms.*," I said automatically.

"This is Detective Ratchet. I am the officer in charge of the Nelsen Nelsen investigation."

I didn't say anything, because I already knew this information.

"I ask that you come to my office this morning to discuss your involvement in yesterday's events."

This was not good news. When you're only a witness, the police ask you *if* you can come talk to them. Also, what involvement? I found a body. Period. My part was passive.

In a businesslike voice, I told him I had time available at ten thirty but would prefer that he come to my office.

It would set a bad precedent if I let this guy push me around at the onset of a case.

Ratchet hesitated and then gave in.

"Fine. I will be at your office at ten thirty."

His tone implied that our appointment time was written in stone and was not to be messed with.

That was fine with me. It gave me another excuse to push back the mom talk.

After I got off the phone, I grabbed a Danish and some coffee and took bites and sips of each, respectively, while I dressed. I went for the no-frills, badass-attorney look and donned a navy pants suit, a white button-down shirt, and medium heels. At the last minute, I added an American flag lapel pin I had gotten free from my plumber for having the highest bill that month.

Later, when I pulled into the small parking lot (née driveway) of my office building, I noticed a Ford Escort with a Hertz sticker parked on the street. It had to be my mother's. Anxiety engulfed me. I came close to turning my little Honda Civic around and slamming my foot down on the accelerator. After a firm lecture by a small group of mature brain cells, however, I did not.

I walked in at ten fifteen, calculating my arrival so as to allow enough time to prepare for Ratchet but not so much time that I could get locked into a conversation with my mother.

I had failed to allow time for shock, however.

The windows were covered by ruffled pink gingham café curtains tied back with bows of wide pink velvet ribbon. Ruffled throw pillows in bright pastels—with pithy messages, such as "Let the sun shine in," "Home is where the heart is," "Love is all you need," and "Smile"—were scattered over the couch and chairs. Matching little white watering cans filled with pink and white silk flowers sat on the end tables, and a large arrangement of silk roses in every shade of pink imaginable occupied center stage on the coffee table. Prints of insufferably adorable children jumping rope, digging in the sand at a beach, and swinging on a swing set hung in a line behind the couch. Fabric samples, pink and white again being the dominant colors, were spread over the couch and chairs. My mother stood in the center of this hellhole, inspecting a swath of flowered fabric draped over the couch. She was, as always, dressed impeccably. She wore light-green pants with a matching sweater accessorized by a green-and-off-white silk scarf and an understated gold necklace and bracelet. Every brown—dyed—hair of her bouffant hairdo was sprayed in place. Her trim figure belied her obsession with chocolate.

Beth looked up from her desk when I came in. She caught my eye and shrugged elaborately. I noticed her cubby had not been affected by the pink explosion and prayed she'd managed to keep my mother away from my office, too.

I took a deep breath. "Hi, Mother."

She turned to face me and clapped her hands in an expression of what innocent bystanders would have interpreted as joy. I knew better. The emotion my mother expressed rarely corresponded to the one she felt.

"I hope you don't mind, dear, but I've taken the liberty of softening the decor in some of the rooms."

Some? That meant the reception area wasn't the only room hit by the ruffle fairy.

The old Kate would have gushed shamelessly and thanked her mother for her kindness and good taste. My mother adored and expected praise. But I'd stopped the false compliments. I had also stopped trying to please her when I had realized the impossibility of the task.

"Mother, we need to have a talk. Are you free for lunch today?"

"Of course! How exciting! I'm so proud of you, sweetie. You are so accomplished and gorgeous, and I'm so thankful you've found some time to spend with me."

I didn't believe a word of it.

The front door opened just as my mother was revving up for another riff of gushing. I turned to see who it was and found myself face-to-face with Webber's doppelgänger. He was a little shorter than Webber but had the same lousy taste in clothes, the same lack of personal hygiene, the same gut hanging over his belt and straining against his shirt buttons, and the same partially bald pate.

"Detective Ratchet?" I asked.

"Yes, and you must be Kate." He shook my hand with a bone-crunching grip. In keeping with my tough-as-nails persona, I kept a neutral expression, even though inside I was screaming in pain.

I suggested we go to my office. En route, I introduced Beth, who grabbed a stack of files to avoid shaking his hand and gave him a smile and a nod instead.

I had to remember that trick.

With another show of Spartan control, I led him to my office and calmly offered him a seat, when, under normal circumstances, I would have collapsed in the doorway.

The reception area was understated by comparison. Where had she found so many ballerina statuettes in such a short time? And the white ruffled rug with the huge, solitary pink peony embroidered in the middle? White lace curtains covered the window, and silk flower arrangements in pink vases were everywhere.

I sat behind my desk, and Ratchet took one of my client chairs after removing a heart-shaped pink velvet pillow.

Over his shoulder, I spotted a gold-framed print of a mother bathing her young daughter in an old-fashioned tub. Both looked healthy and happy.

I moved two porcelain ballerinas out of the way and folded my hands on my desk, which was covered with a pink sateen tablecloth.

"May I move this?" asked Ratchet, pointing to a massive vase filled with fake lilies of the valley and roses that blocked his view of me.

I grabbed the vase and set in on the floor.

"Much better," he said. "Now, could you tell me how you strangled Mr. Nelsen and then hung his body in that building?"

Ratchet was using the oldest trick in the book: try to shock the witness, and hope for a telling reaction.

Bryan had tipped me off, though, so I was prepared.

I looked at Ratchet with an expression of controlled surprise. "How did he die?" I asked.

"Are you saying you had nothing to do with his death?" countered Ratchet with a raised eyebrow and exaggerated sarcasm.

I wasn't taking the bait. Ratchet was not going to control this interview.

"I saw what looked like a hanging body. I called the police. Period. End of involvement."

"Aren't you leaving something out?"

"The police took their sweet time getting there, and they didn't seem overly interested until they discovered the body was that of a white person."

Ratchet's bulldog face hardened, and his eyes narrowed. I looked at him calmly.

"We have information that you knew Mr. Nelsen."

"Mr. Nelsen was sitting in a tree in the backyard of a house I toured. I spoke with him then and again later, when I went to take another look at the house."

I explained about Nelsen and the UFO.

"Why did you go to South Phoenix to find his building?"

I told him about Nelsen's children and my subsequent curiosity about his life. The explanation sounded lame even to me.

"Isn't it true he threatened to file a claim for adverse possession in the event you purchased the house?"

Ratchet had done his homework—I'd give him that. He must have already spoken to Jane.

"I have not made up my mind about the house. Why would I care about a claim unless I had already committed to purchase the house?"

"Why would you care about Nelsen at all then? *You're* the one who went to the old bakery building."

There was no short answer to that question. One had to know me. I feel responsible for, and the need to protect, every living thing that wanders into my orbit. This is why I never go to animal shelters. The cost of all the adoptions would break me.

Nelsen had been estranged from his family and living part-time in a tree, and as far as I was concerned, he might as well have been an inmate at the dog pound.

A tear rolled out of the corner of my eye. The tear was not part of the plan, so I hastily wiped it away.

"Allergies," I commented.

"Why did you go?" persisted Ratchet.

"I told you. I was concerned about Nelsen. He was living in a homeless shelter. I wanted to find out if he had any assets he could sell so he could move to a better place."

"Believe it," said a voice from the hallway. Since the walls in my office are paper thin, whomever was standing out there didn't need to be in my office to be in on the conversation.

The door opened, and Detective Webber stepped in. He was wearing jeans and a bright yellow sweatshirt that said *My Daughter's a Cheerleader*.

Ratchet and I asked in unison, with the same level of dismay, "What are you doing here?"

"Nice sweatshirt," Ratchet added.

"I heard about the Nelsen case, and since I know the chief witness pretty damn well, I thought I'd drop by to help." Webber entered uninvited and took a chair. It was then that he noticed the change in decor.

"This place looks like the inside of a Pepto-Bismol bottle. What the hell happened in here?"

I groaned and placed a hand over my forehead. "My mother is visiting, and she redecorated."

"Your mother? Is she the one stapling ruffles to the couch in the reception area?"

I groaned again. The couch was leather.

I felt a flash of concern. "Where is Beth?"

Beth is a tartan when it comes to visitors, such as Webber, who drop in without appointments. No one gets in to see me unless he or she has scheduled an appointment.

"She's outside sitting on the front steps, smoking," said Webber, picking up one of the ballerina statuettes and examining it suspiciously.

He probably couldn't wrap his mind around the idea of my owning such an object unless it had a nefarious purpose.

I took it from him and placed it outside his reach. "Beth doesn't smoke," I said.

"She does now," said Webber with a shrug. "Unfiltered."

Sam smoked unfiltered cigarettes from time to time. She must have gotten into his stash.

I guessed Mother had been at it again. "Was Beth crying?"

"No, but she was mumbling something about a wasted life. She didn't even notice when I walked by."

"You're supposed to be on vacation having fun, Webber," Ratchet interrupted, sensing he was losing control of the interview.

"Vacation—ha! I was at my kid's cheerleading camp. Nothin' fun about it. I was relieved as hell when they told me to go home."

"Why were you told to leave?"

Webber shifted his gaze to a print of a cherubic little kid sitting on a chamber pot. "A bunch of creepers were showing up every day to watch the girls practice, so I asked a friend in the Flagstaff PD to check 'em out while I went undercover and did some questioning. Turns out they were other parents, and they took exception to the investigation.

"Technically, I have another week of vacation left, but I'm willing to use my remaining time to help out on the Nelsen case."

Ratchet rubbed his temples. Beads of sweat had popped out on his forehead.

"I think you'd better go through the office on this one, Fred."

"Who's Fred?" I blurted.

"That's his first name," said Ratchet, jerking his head toward Webber.

Amazingly, until then, I had never heard Webber referred to as anything other than Detective Webber, Webber, asshole, or jerk. (Okay, those last two were mine.)

"Already talked to the captain," said Webber. "He's thrilled to have a senior detective with my background on the case."

"Did he appoint you as lead?" asked Ratchet resignedly. Apparently, the captain hadn't thought to include Ratchet in the decision-making process.

"No, you're still chief on this one. I'm more like a consultant."

Ratchet looked better after hearing this, but he shouldn't have. No way would Webber keep to the role of a consultant.

I looked exaggeratedly at my watch—or I would have if I'd remembered to put it on that morning. "Are we through here, gentlemen?"

Ratchet closed the notebook he had taken out at the beginning of his interview and put it inside an oddly feminine pink- and blue-striped cloth carryall.

"For now," he said. "I will want to speak with you again after I confer with Detective Webber, however."

"Please talk to my secretary, Beth, to schedule any further interviews," I said tersely, making the point that my time was valuable and he'd better follow protocol from there on out. Of course, this was assuming I could pry the cigarette out of Beth's hand and get her back to her desk.

I waited until I heard Ratchet and Webber drive off before I left my office. I passed my mother on the way through the reception area, but thankfully, she was too busy tacking fake flowers around the windows to notice.

Beth was still sitting on the front steps. She was smoking and, judging by the pile of cigarette butts on the ground next to her, had been hard at it for a while. Her brown complexion looked muddy, and her eyes were red—both symptoms of the amateur smoker.

I sat next to her and got to the point. "Why are you out here smoking?"

Beth tapped off an inch-long ash and studied her fingers carefully. "I wanted to think about some things," she answered ambiguously.

She'd probably had a relapse after my mini pep-talk that morning. "Is it something my mother said?"

Beth gave me a sidelong glance and then nodded miserably.

"Beth, don't listen to anything she says. You are a wonderful, worthwhile person. I don't know what I would do without you—not just because you're the world's best assistant but because you're a good friend and an amazing human being."

Beth was back to the finger staring. "It's not about me. It's about you."

"Me?" I asked in surprise. "What do you mean?"

"I think maybe you should ask your mom about it. She told me some things that were hard to hear about you. But you need to handle it between the two of you. I'd like to know the truth of it, but it's not my business."

"The truth of what? Tell me, Beth."

But she clamped her mouth into a thin line and shook her head.

I felt a flash of anger toward my mother—or, more correctly, a spike of anger, since I always harbored some level of anger toward her.

I patted Beth's shoulder sympathetically. I, more than anyone, understood that being an innocent bystander in the drama of my mother's life was uncomfortable.

I rose to my feet and went back inside to accost the perpetrator of Beth's misery.

"Mother, I need to ask you to keep your communications with my staff at a minimum, and by 'minimum,' I mean do not speak to any of them unless it is a red-level emergency, such as you being on fire or having a stroke, and by 'stroke,' I do not mean transient ischemia. I mean a hardcore, can't-remember-your-name-or-feel-your-body stroke."

Without waiting for a response, I quickstepped to my office.

CHAPTER 6

I buzzed Sam on our seldom-used intercom—shouting was easier but not as classy—and asked him to come to my office and bring MJ with him.

Minutes later, they walked in and sat on my two client chairs. Both looked at me expectantly.

I noticed Sam was not wearing his high heels, probably for my mother's benefit, but MJ had not toned down her wardrobe one iota. Today she had jammed her impressive bulk into a stretchy—although not stretchy enough—shiny blue dress that barely covered her bottom, sheer black nylons covered with vaguely sinister skulls, and Doc Martens. The dress was sleeveless, so her tattooed arms were available for public inspection, and she had replaced her regular, smaller nose ring with a large gold hoop. MJ is a conscientious color coordinator, so her hair was dyed the same shade of blue as her dress. MJ, at forty-three, was not going gently into that good night.

"Nice dress," I commented.

"I know, right? It's just like one Kate Middleton wore."

Sam raised an eyebrow. "Didn't they have it in your size?"

"Screw you. It fits like a glove," snapped MJ.

"A latex glove."

I smacked my palm on the desk. "Enough, you two. We have a new case to talk about."

"A new case we're getting paid for or a Kate case?" asked Sam.

Kate case is office code for "We are working for free."

"The latter," I said briskly.

They groaned in unison.

I told them about George Booker and his flock and the possibility that since Nelsen's death was now classified as murder, we would be representing a member of his flock in the investigation. I then briefly outlined what Reverend Booker had told me.

"I don't think there's much chance the police will consider any of them suspects," commented MJ. "What's their motive?"

Sam grunted. "They're black, and they live in South Phoenix. That's the only motive the police need."

"Come on. It's the twenty-first century," scoffed MJ. "That kind of prejudice is long gone."

I shook my head ruefully. "I hate to agree with Sam on this one, but it's true. The rules are different for folks down there."

"But the percentage of cops who are people of color has increased. Even they are prejudiced?"

"It's part of the police culture. No one is immune. Remember that whole mess about a month ago, when off-duty police were hired to provide security for a development in South Phoenix, and even though they were paid, they didn't perform the services? They got away with it for a long time. They could never pull something like that in North Scottsdale."

"If you're black and poor, not much has changed," added Sam.

As if on cue, the phone rang, and my caller ID identified the caller as George Booker.

I answered, and the deep voice of the reverend reverberated over the line. After we exchanged greetings, he said, "It's started."

I told him my staff was with me, and I asked permission to put him on speakerphone. He gave me the go-ahead, and I successfully pulled off the technology portion of our meeting. After introductions were made, Reverend Booker filled us in.

"This morning, the police paid visits to Deacon Davis and Deacon Washington with warrants to search their houses. They found a baggie of marijuana in Deacon Davis's son's room and arrested Deacon Davis for possession. They didn't find anything in Deacon Washington's house, but after the police left, he got a call from the city about a zoning violation in his backyard."

"Have you been contacted yet?" I asked.

"No, but I haven't answered the phone today."

"Do you know why they questioned Deacon Davis and Deacon Washington?"

"It's because they were the ones cleaning up the old bakery. The police must have found their fingerprints."

"That means their prints were already in the system," commented Sam. "Do you know why?"

"Both Deacon Davis and Deacon Washington spent time in prison a long time ago. I don't remember why."

I took a big breath. "Reverend Booker, please advise the members of your congregation that they are to call me in the event they are contacted by the police. The same advice goes for you. In the meantime, I'll meet with Deacon Davis. If the police arrest Deacon Washington, I will find him an attorney. Do you know which jail Deacon Davis was taken to?"

"The Fourth Avenue jail," he said in a tone that implied he had experience with that particular institution.

The Fourth Avenue jail was operated by the sheriff's office, and the holding cells were small, crowded, and smelly. No effort was made to separate the truly violent from the balance of the jail population.

I left MJ and Sam to explain our office policies to Reverend Booker and then headed out. Getting Deacon Davis out of the Fourth Avenue jail was a priority. His safety was at stake.

As I rushed through the reception area, my mother jumped off the couch and looked at me hopefully. "Are we going to lunch now?"

"Something's come up. I have to go to jail," I said abruptly.

My mother gripped her throat with both hands. "God no! I *knew* something like this was bound to happen."

"To see a client, Mother. I'll be back in about an hour, if you want to wait."

"May I come with?"

"*No.*"

No one would survive unscathed from a jail visit by my mother. Prisoners and personnel would be placed on suicide watch after she left.

I raced to my car, threw myself into the front seat, and hit the door locks in case she decided to more aggressively pursue the idea. My hands shook as I started the car.

Stop it. You're not a child anymore, lectured the adult portion of my brain.

The front door of my office building opened, and reason disappeared. *Leave,* commanded my inner child.

Stepping hard on the gas, I backed out of the driveway like a NASCAR driver.

I managed to get my anxiety under control by the time I reached the jail and pulled into one of the city's overpriced parking spaces. The meter costs were so high that it almost made sense to book a hotel room in the area and take advantage of the free hotel parking.

I paid my pound of flesh and went through the jail's visitor entrance. I remembered to take out my ID and leave my purse in the car, which would expedite the security check. I had learned the hard way that a security check of my handbag not only wasted time but also required that I endure raised eyebrows and embarrassing questions, such as, "Why do you have a can of Sterno, Christmas ornaments, and Mardi Gras beads in your purse?"

I handed my business card to the deputy at the front desk and requested an interview with Tamir Makai Davis (Deacon Davis's full name). I also requested and received a copy of his arraignment notice. The arraignment was set for nine o'clock the next morning.

I took a seat on a plastic chair in a white-walled waiting room that smelled of bleach. Three other attorneys were waiting to be called once deputies delivered their clients to interview rooms. I estimated I had at least a thirty-minute wait. Since I hadn't brought anything to read, the only form of entertainment available to me was listening to the conversations floating around the room. I wasn't nosy—just bored.

The man dressed in the shiny dark blue polyester suit with a light pink shirt and darker pink tie was Ron Schecter, an attorney with Lozer and Fry, a local criminal law firm that specialized in DUI defense. Since DUI cases are cookie cutter (that is, sentencing is restricted by statute), the defense attorney's primary functions are hand-holding and shoulder patting, no special training required. DUI firms make money based on quantity, not quality, of representation. While this area of practice is lucrative, I would rather work in a third-world sweatshop, the latter being more intellectually challenging.

I didn't recognize the man with whom Schecter was talking, but the plastic ID hanging from the cord around his neck identified him as a staff member of the county prosecutor's office. He was likely there to talk to a witness.

The third attorney was also someone I did not recognize. He was good looking in a Colin Firth kind of way, and I tagged him as a public defender because of his corduroy jacket and khakis. I had to cut my observations short, though, because he was looking at me, and each time I glanced in his direction, our eyes met in one of those awkward "Hey, we're looking at each other" moments.

"Hi, Kate," said Schecter. "What brings you to the happiest place on earth?"

"What else? I've got a client in there," I said, jerking my head toward the door that led back to the cells.

"Hello," said the guy with the county badge, reaching out to shake my hand. "Dale Farnham."

"And I am Mike Raymond," said the man in the corduroy jacket.

"Kate Williams," I said during one-pump handshakes with both.

"I've heard of you," said Dale.

At least he was polite enough to leave it at that and not go into detail.

"So what did your client do?"

"*Allegedly* do," corrected Schecter.

"So what did your guy *allegedly* do?" asked Dale.

"Possession of less than an ounce of marijuana," I said, leaving out the possible-suspicion-of-murder part.

"Not bad," said Schecter. "Cases like that are quick turnarounds. Mike here is screwed, though. He pulled a murder one. No vacation for Mike anytime soon."

"My plane tickets and hotel reservations are refundable," he responded. "In this business, you never go hard on vacation plans."

I nodded sympathetically. A trial attorney's life is governed by statutes and judges' schedules. We have little to say about when and for how long we will be in court.

"Are you with the public defender's office?" I asked, looking to confirm my original assumption.

"No. I'm with Jones and Ralston, out of Los Angeles."

Whoa. Jones and Ralston was one of the largest firms in Los Angeles and had a reputation for playing hardball. Whomever had hired Mike had money.

I experienced a wave of envy and wondered what it would be like to have a well-paying client—or even a paying client.

"You must be here on a high-profile case," I commented.

He smiled. "Not for long, if I can help it. I'm going to do my best to get my client out of this as quickly as possible."

"Who did your guy pull for his preliminary hearing?" asked Schecter.

"Judge Wiener."

Schecter and Dale snorted. "I hope you booked a hotel room," said Ray. "You're not going anywhere for a while. Judge Wiener is an ex-prosecutor and has never let a murder-one suspect out on bail that I'm aware of."

Mike didn't seem disturbed by this information and continued to smile benignly.

"Kate, your guy is in room two," said the deputy at the desk.

"Hey," groused Schecter. "We've been here longer than she has."

I smiled sweetly and waved bye-bye.

It helps to have connections.

I passed through the door and walked down a long, fluorescent-lit hall to room number two, which, for reasons known only to the county facilities manager, was located between rooms five and seven.

Inside room two, a large black man with short, cropped gray hair was seated on the other side of the Plexiglas barrier that separated counsel from client. Phones hung on the wall on either side, but an intercom rendered use of the phones unnecessary.

"Deacon Davis, I've been asked by Reverend Booker to represent you. Are you okay with that plan?"

He nodded and stared at me expressionlessly.

"You're presently charged with possession of less than one ounce of marijuana, which is a misdemeanor. Do you know why the officer booked you in jail instead of citing and releasing you?"

"I got two priors," he said, not moving his eyes from mine.

"Drug related?"

He nodded.

Arizona had a three-strikes rule, so this was serious business. Felony charges could be filed, and prison time was a certainty. I explained all this, but the deacon's lack of reaction led me to believe he was already aware of his circumstances.

"Did the police question you about the death of Mr. Nelsen?"

He nodded again.

Getting him to talk was like pulling teeth.

"Mr. Davis, do you understand that I'm on your side? Anything you tell me is privileged."

"I been through this before. I know you gonna try your best. I also know how it's gonna come out—I get to be a guest of the state of Arizona again."

"Mr. Davis, you need to tell me what happened. You have been charged with possession of a controlled substance, and it's also possible the police will bring charges against you for the murder of Mr. Nelsen."

That got his attention.

"What for? I ain't seen Mr. Nelsen, God bless his soul, since the late nineties on the day before he shut down the bakery. I was his night manager. I ain't been able to find full-time work since."

"Reverend Booker thinks the police found your prints inside the bakery."

"Mine and a bunch of others. That don't mean nothin'. That buildin's been used as a drug house on and off since the business closed. Rev'rand Booker prob'ly told you what we was tryin' to do over there. I been in there with Deacon Washington every day the last few months, makin' plans and tryin' to clean up some of the mess. Most of the elders and other deacons has been there too, doin' the same thing.

"I go in at night sometimes because some of the old drug crowd shows up from time to time, an' if we don't catch 'em, they get up to their bad business again."

"You mean the building is still used for criminal activities?" I asked.

"Yep. And also by some of the high-school kids when they want to mess around."

I remembered the condoms I had seen on the floor. I couldn't think of a less-romantic place for messing around.

It was odd that the police would home in on deacons Washington and Davis. The place must have been loaded with other people's prints.

"Have you been on the third floor of the building?" I asked.

"Yes, ma'am. That's the only floor we got cleaned up so far. It wasn't as bad as the first and second floors. I guess junkies is too lazy to climb steps."

That had to be it: the police had narrowed their focus to prints found on the third floor. Still, they hadn't arrested either Deacon Davis or Deacon Washington for the murder yet, so they did not have enough evidence to file charges. They were just trying to keep Davis where they could find him and were doubtless keeping an eye on Deacon Washington, too.

I explained what I was thinking to Deacon Davis.

He shrugged. "If that's all they got, they got nothin'. They ain't gonna find any evidence that I so much as touched Mr. Nelsen, much less kilt him."

The drug charge, however, was a different issue.

"Mr. Davis, the police report says the marijuana you were picked up for was found in your son's room. Is it possible the drugs were his?"

He clamped his lips together and shook his head. It was clear he wasn't going to implicate his son.

"Your son isn't part of this at all then. I see."

"He's a good boy. He's gonna go to college. I don't want him to have no record."

I explained that since his son was a minor with no priors, he would get probation at most, and the conviction would not show up on his record.

He still refused to implicate his son.

"It's psychological," he said. "I don't want him gettin' it in his head that he's a druggie. I don't want him goin' down that path."

I wondered how his son's psychology would be impacted by his dad going back to prison.

I asked Mr. Davis a few questions relevant to his arraignment, including whether he had money for bail or other assets he could pledge to a bail bondsman—he had a total of $105 and rented his home—and told him I would meet him in court tomorrow for his appearance.

If Mr. Davis wasn't going to help himself, then my staff and I had a lot of work to do. Also, the way things were stacking up against him, it was unlikely that I could get Deacon Davis released on a $100 bond, but I would give it my best shot.

Mike was still sitting in the outer office when I left. The other two men were gone.

"Have you seen your client yet?" I asked.

He shook his head. "If I didn't know better, I'd say the local constabulary doesn't like out-of-towners."

I laughed. "So far as I know, they feel the same level of animosity toward all defense attorneys."

"I heard you have connections, though. Schecter said you and the sheriff are tight. Any chance you can speed up the process for me?"

I blushed a deep red but kept my voice steady. "I assure you Sheriff Turner would never grant me a courtesy not available to all attorneys dealing with his office."

Just then, the deputy at the desk announced that Mike's client, Nelsen Nelsen, was waiting in room seven.

I froze upon hearing the name but thawed quickly enough to grab Mike's arm before he could leave the room.

"There was a man by that name recently murdered in this town," I said.

"Yes, I know. My client is the deceased's son, Nelsen Nelsen Jr."

"He's been accused of his father's murder?"

"He was the last one to see his father alive, according to the police. I disagree and believe the court will side with my client. The senior Mr. Nelsen was found in a disagreeable part of town in a building known to be used as a drug house. One of the local junkies likely came in and killed Nelsen Senior after my client left."

I got the feeling Deacon Davis was the police's top pick for the role of drug-crazed junkie.

I wished Mike luck, crossing my fingers behind my back.

I strategized Deacon Davis's defense on the way back to my office. The first step was to get MJ and Sam started on a thorough background check of Davis, Nelsen Jr., and Nelsen Sr. Sam would also have the task of getting what information he could out of the police and prosecutor's offices. Sam had been an investigator for the county attorney's office for ten years before I hired him, and he still had contacts on the inside.

We didn't have time for the discovery process to run its course. We had to make our move before the police and Mike honed in on my client as a scapegoat, if they hadn't already.

The urgency surrounding Davis's case drove out thoughts of my mother. This state of relative nirvana vanished as soon as I walked through the front door of my office building.

My mother was lying in wait in the reception area. She jumped up from the couch and blocked my path.

"Time for lunch," she announced merrily.

"I'm really sorry, Mother, but we have a bit of an emergency. Can we reschedule?"

She deflated dramatically. "Of course! I'm just an old woman with nothing to do, hoping her daughter will pay her a little attention. Don't worry about *my* silly schedule. Let's just plan it for whenever you have a moment."

"Great. Thanks," I said, pretending to take her words at face value but knowing full well that my mother never meant anything she said literally.

On the way to my office, I banged on MJ's and Sam's doors and asked them to come see me as soon as they could. By the time I was seated behind my desk, both of them had come in and, after a brief shoving match over who sat where, settled in across from me.

MJ pretended to be fascinated by the pink satin tablecloth on my desk.

"I'm gonna get one of these," she said.

I winced.

"Shut up, MJ," ordered Sam. "Can't you see this is a sore subject for Kate? Although honestly, I think pastels would be better than your current choice. Your office looks like the inside of a coffin, except for the fluorescent posters of Nirvana and Garth Brooks.

"By the way, where the hell did you find that poster of Garth Brooks? He's a cowboy country-western singer, and fluorescence doesn't seem—"

"Focus, you two," I interrupted. "As for my office's new decor, it goes as soon as my mother leaves."

Speaking loudly to drown out MJ's request for my big-eyed children pictures, I explained what had happened at the jail and my suspicion that Deacon Davis was about to become the focus of a murder investigation.

"Wasn't Nelsen Jr. the guy you saw when you were in the tree with Nelsen Sr.?" asked MJ.

"How did you know about that?" I didn't recall mentioning the incident to my staff.

"Some pushy broad named Jane called this morning and told me about it. She said she realized it was difficult to talk to you with the Nelsens there yesterday and wanted to schedule a time today to discuss your home purchase. Did you find a house?"

"Maybe, but I don't have time for that now. As for the man I saw yesterday, unless there is more than one Nelsen Nelsen Jr., he's sitting in jail, charged with his father's murder.

"Nelsen Sr. said he wanted time to think before he talked to his children. I guess he decided to meet to his son at least. Mike, Nelsen Jr.'s attorney, said dad and son were together at the old bakery yesterday.

"That reminds me. Sam, we'll need to interview people in the area surrounding the bakery to find out if anyone saw a person or persons around the bakery building on the day of the murder."

Sam snorted. "I doubt we'll get much cooperation. Those people don't want anything to do with the legal process. As far as they're concerned, any involvement never turns out well."

"I thought you said you haven't been down there much?"

"I don't need to be. Every Phoenix cop knows how it works down there, and I heard plenty about it when I worked at the county attorney's office."

I was offended by the racial overtones of Sam's assessment and his use of the term "those people," and I told him so.

He responded sarcastically, "The lovely folks in SoPho have had unfortunate experiences with the legal process and so tend to be closed mouthed."

"Fine. I'll do the interviews."

"You can't go down there alone."

"I'll go with you," volunteered MJ.

"Thank you, MJ," I said.

She raised her eyebrows and gave Sam a Kate-likes-me-better look.

Sam rolled his eyes. "We'll all go. It's safer that way."

"You make it sound like Iraq, you big wuss," grumbled MJ.

"Tomorrow then—after the arraignment. If everything goes well, Deacon Davis can come with us," I said. "Now, let's get cracking on the background checks."

CHAPTER 7

We all "got cracking"—it was a term I'd never understood, but it seemed to get the point across.

I was absorbed in preparations for the arraignment, which normally would have been pro forma but might take a hard turn in this case, so I didn't look at the caller ID when my mobile phone rang. I absently picked up.

"Katie, it's Jane."

I stifled a groan.

"Jane, I don't have time—"

"This won't take but a second. I just thought you'd like to know that the seller of the Arcadia house has reduced the price by fifty thousand. It's sure to sell quickly now. I just wanted to let you know before someone else snaps it up."

Part of me knew that the threat of another purchaser was a ploy to create a false sense of urgency, but the part of me that really wanted the house fell for it.

"Well, maybe I can come by and take another look at it sometime."

"See you at the house at five thirty then," said Jane. She hung up before I had a chance to say anything.

I looked at my watch. It was already four thirty. I rationalized that I could limit the house visit to thirty minutes and still have time to complete the rest of my work at home.

I spent the next half hour collecting files for Deacon Davis's arraignment and a couple cases with motions due the next day and then headed out. Thankfully, my mother was gone, so I didn't have to leave through the back window.

I arrived at the Arcadia house early. The short commute was impressive. Because I didn't have to deal with a parking garage and elevator, it actually took less time door to door than it took to get to my condo.

I got out of my car and sat on the front step to wait for Jane.

Several people, most of them likely just home from work, were out walking their dogs, and a group of kids were riding their bikes in the cul-de-sac. The area had a safe feel to it.

One of the dog walkers accidently dropped the leash of his dachshund as he bent over to pick up a newspaper. The dog shot off in my direction. Before I could get to my feet, she was in my lap, washing my face with her tongue. Something on me must have been delicious, because she really went at it. Maybe it was my Estee Lauder antiaging liquid makeup. (I had bought it after the saleswoman insisted it reversed the signs of aging. It didn't.)

"Heidi! Heidi!" called her owner, a well-built young man of about eighteen or nineteen.

Heidi ignored him and started licking my arm. Once I got past the thought of where dogs stick their tongues when they're not licking people, I kind of enjoyed it.

The young man swore under his breath and trotted toward us.

"Sorry," he said, sounding more annoyed than sorry. "It's my mother's dog."

He pulled Heidi roughly off my lap as she yelped in protest.

"It's all right, really." I reached up and stroked Heidi's head so that she knew there were no hard feelings. "She must have smelled my dog. Do you live around here?"

"There," he said, pointing to the house across the street.

"Do you go to school nearby?"

"Yeah. Arcadia High School. I'm a senior. Listen, lady, I don't have time to chitchat. I need to take Heidi home and get to football practice."

I watched as he strode across the street, holding Heidi out in front of him as if she were radioactive, and then disappeared into the house.

I unsuccessfully tried to dismiss the young man's rudeness as a function of youth and lack of social graces. I thought he was a jerk, and I did not like how he treated Heidi.

Jane pulled into the driveway and tooted her horn merrily. I gave her a wave and got to my feet.

"Have you been waiting long?" she asked as soon as she was out of her car.

"No. I got here early to get the feel of the neighborhood. I met the young man who lives across the street and the family dog."

"You met Chad?"

"He didn't introduce himself, but he's a big kid and said he's a senior in high school."

"That's Chad. He's the Trojans' quarterback. He's a tad full of himself."

"Do you know the family?" I asked curiously. Jane didn't strike me as the type who went out of her way to meet anyone not directly involved in real-estate sales.

"Yes. Chad has a bit of a temper. My car was parked in the driveway while I was showing the house about a week ago. He backed his truck out of his driveway too fast and hit my car's back bumper. He called me the B word and said it was my fault. We had a real screaming match on the front lawn. But then his mom came over, and she was so kind and apologetic. She and her husband paid for the repairs to my car out of pocket because they didn't want to report the incident to their insurance company."

Realizing this might not be an effective sales pitch, she added, "His mom says it's a phase. Anyway, Chad will be going to college next year and won't be around much after that."

I followed Jane into the house and felt the same sense of welcome I'd experienced before. This house definitely liked me. I was drawn to the window and looked out sadly at Nelsen's tree.

Jane came up quietly behind me. "Sad, isn't it? The police called me about it this morning. His son told them his father hung out here."

It was an unfortunate choice of words.

I looked through the house again but this time avoided the backyard. The late-afternoon sun streaming through the windows gave the home's interior a soft glow. How could such a peaceful place have such a tragic history?

Before I left, I took the residential-purchase agreement form Jane handed me and told her I would think about it.

I headed to my car, and a late-model black Toyota truck screeched around the corner and pulled into the driveway of the house across the street. The truck was equipped with every accessory Toyota offered: chrome fog lamps, grill, and bumpers and wide tires. Rap music blared from a sound system that rivaled that of an IMAX theater.

Chad hopped out of his truck, and a woman emerged from the house. She was about my age, with long dark hair pulled back into a ponytail. She was slim almost to the point of emaciation, and the curve of her shoulders and stiff movements suggested the possibility of early onset osteoporosis. The tracksuit she wore hung from her sharp bones in folds. The overall impression she gave was one of extreme frailty.

She placed her hand on Chad's arm and said something I couldn't hear, but her speech had the tenor of a question. He shook off her hand and strode into the house without reply.

The woman looked in my direction, and I quickly looked away, embarrassed that I had been caught watching them.

"Hello!" she called out.

I waved politely in return.

"I've seen your car here before. Are you thinking of buying that house?" she asked, walking toward me.

"Perhaps. It's a lovely house," I said noncommittally.

A smile lit up her face, transforming her into a real beauty.

"I hope you do. The house needs people who care about it."

It was odd that she said this, because that was exactly how I felt.

We exchanged introductions. Her name was Nancy Alport.

"Did you know the people who lived here before?" I asked.

Her smile immediately faded. "Yes. A lovely family. What happened to their daughter is so sad. My Chad went to school with her and was at the party the night she died. The kids took her death hard."

"Were you at home when it happened?" I asked.

"No, no. My husband and I were at a restaurant, having dinner with the Jacobs—Tiffany's parents. You know how kids are. They must have decided it was a good night for a party, with Tiffany's parents out of the house. When we got home, the police and EMTs were here. That strange little man who sits in the tree called them. The kids hadn't noticed that Tiffany was in trouble. They thought she was just kidding around."

"You mean Nelsen called the police?" I asked with surprise.

"Yes. You've met Nelsen?"

"I met him a couple of days ago. We had a nice talk in the tree." I paused, not sure if I should go on. I didn't know how well she had known Nelsen and didn't want to be the bearer of bad news.

"How nice. I got the feeling he didn't have a lot of friends. I was sorry to hear he died."

So she did know, and she didn't seem particularly sorry. In fact, she seemed distracted and kept glancing nervously over her shoulder.

The front door opened, and Chad glared at us from its threshold.

"Mom, where's dinner? I gotta get moving. Jake and I are going to a movie in an hour."

"But, Chad, it's a school night. I don't think—"

Chad slammed the door.

Nancy smiled ruefully and shrugged. "Teens can be so demanding."

I had another word for it but didn't say it.

"My husband, Kevin, is a contractor at Luke Air Force Base, and he's not home much. It's too bad, because I think Chad would benefit from having a male role model."

Or a parole officer, I thought.

"I'd better go feed him before he throws a tantrum. It was nice meeting you, Kate. I hope you'll be our new neighbor."

I was tempted to ask if her son was planning to attend an out-of-state college. Chad was more of a negative than Nelsen had been, as far as I was concerned.

Instead, I smiled and expressed my pleasure at having met her—and only her.

CHAPTER 8

As I drove away, I mentally patted myself on the back for deciding against having children. Detective Webber's daughter, Emily, was a delight, of course, but there was no guarantee one would end up with an Emily.

My mother, however, had never forgiven me for not having children. You'd think my sister's three daughters would have satisfied her grandmother quota, but in each of our infrequent conversations, she reminded me of how I had failed her in this as well as many other areas.

Feeling the need for companionship, I called Tuwanda and asked if she wanted to go to dinner, which, in Tuwanda's world, was an early lunch. She thought that was a grand idea, and we made plans to meet at Houston's in a half hour, giving me just enough time to go home to walk and feed Ralph. I thought about how great it would be to have a yard so that all I had to do was open the door and let him out. Maybe I would get a doggy door and eliminate the need for even that slight effort.

The wait at Houston's was twenty minutes, so we had time for a drink on the outdoor patio before being seated. A rowdy bunch of baseball fans in town for the Diamondbacks-versus-Cardinals game made conversation on the patio difficult, but we were shown to a quiet table for dinner, where we could hear each other without screaming.

Tuwanda brought me up to date on business, letting me know to expect a couple of new cases the next day because the police were cracking down on her Care Bares again. Dragnets such as this were typical right before elections. Then we moved to the topic of the Arcadia house that I now called, at least in my mind, my house.

I told her about meeting Chad and Nancy and said I was going to make an offer despite the negative karma of a drowning, an alien abduction, and the brat across the street.

"I don' know, Kate. It seems to me with your lifestyle bein' the way it is, you'd want someplace with a clean slate, so to speak."

My need to save the house was too complicated and too weird to explain, so I said nothing.

"Wait a minute! I got a good idea! Why don' you ask Venus to do an exorcism?"

I'd met Venus Butterrman when I represented her grandson in a murder case. Venus claims she can communicate with the dead and, although I remain skeptical, has come up with information on cases that seemingly could only have come from the deceased victim.

"Can she do exorcisms? I thought only priests could do that kind of thing," I said doubtfully.

"It don' hurt to ask. Even if she can't kick 'em out, she can at least tell you if you got spirits hangin' around. Could be there ain't even any of 'em there."

I didn't think it mattered either way, but I knew how much Tuwanda loved Venus's séances, so I was willing to go along, provided I could work it into my schedule.

"Can you imagine Jane's reaction when I insist on acceptable results from a séance as a condition to buying the house?"

We laughed at the thought. Of course, I would include no such provision, because aside from being unenforceable, knowing Jane, she would demand to be present at the séance and would interfere with Venus's conjuring skills—not that she had any.

After lunch, before parting ways, Tuwanda made me call Venus and leave a voice mail about scheduling a séance.

Once back at my condo, I decided to defer my legal work and settled in to draft an offer to purchase the Arcadia house, feeling good about my decision and excited about the prospect of owning the house.

The phone rang as I was wading through the agreement's warranties and representations. Assuming it was Venus, I picked up without checking the caller ID.

"Kate?"

I was caught off guard and responded more brusquely than was perhaps polite. "Mother, what do you want?"

"I'm sorry. If you're in the middle of something important, I can call back. Or even better, just give me a call when you have time, dear."

I sighed. "No, it's fine, Mother."

"I just wanted to know if we are going to lunch tomorrow."

"I'm sorry about today. Tomorrow would be fine."

"Wonderful! I'm so pleased! I'll just call Darlene and let her know I can't meet her for lunch."

"Darlene?"

"Yes. Don't you remember Darlene? We were Kappa Deltas together in college. She married Dewey Witt—you know, the CEO of Westingford International? At least he was until he retired. Now they just travel to their homes in Edina and Carefree and their castle in England. They're in Carefree, and of course, the first thing she did was call me for lunch."

"Mother, if you have other plans, we can put our lunch off until the following day."

"Oh no, dear. Having lunch with you is more important than seeing Darlene. She will be upset, of course. She looks forward to our lunches so much."

"Mother, if you want to go to lunch with Darlene, it's okay with me."

"No, dear. You are my lovely daughter, and I want to be with you, although Darlene is leaving for England the day after tomorrow, so she won't be able to see me for a while."

"Please go to lunch with Darlene."

"Well, if you prefer that I did."

"I prefer it."

After we hung up, I felt drained. My mother could make an ordeal out of something as simple as scheduling lunch. I had just spent five minutes of my life I would never get back. The upside was that our lunch was delayed yet another day.

I put off the rest of the contract review until the next day, worked for a couple of hours, and then went to bed. My dreams were filled with images of drowning children and hanging people. In one sequence, Chad chased me through Nelsen's bakery, which then turned into my childhood home, where my mother joined Chad in the chase. My clock's alarm came as a relief when it went off at 6:00 a.m.—so much so that I did not pound the off button with my usual misdirected hostility.

I was at the court by eight thirty and took a seat in the back of the galley to wait until Deacon Davis's case was called. The courtroom was one of the older ones with scuffed wood pews, bad fluorescent lighting, and dark paneling. It smelled like a combination of old books, floor wax, and sweat.

The attorney handling the arraignments for the state was Tom Young, a lifer in his fifties who had lost his sense of humor decades ago.

I spotted Mike Raymond sitting in the front row. He turned to scan the room and gave me a friendly wave when he saw me.

Judge Weiner took the bench at nine o'clock sharp, which was unusual for him. I guessed his timeliness was inspired by the presence of several members of the press in the courtroom.

The bailiff barked, "All rise," and we all stood as one and waited as Weiner took the bench. It took him a few minutes to negotiate the three steps up to the bench, as he was impeded by age, a bad knee, and innate clumsiness. He tripped on the last step and disappeared behind the bench. We heard scuffling noises, and then his head popped up. He peered down at us peons. His struggle with gravity evidenced only by a small cut on his forehead, he slammed the gavel against the desk, missing the block by a good foot. Taking our cue, we all sat.

The bailiff called the first case on the calendar: the arraignment of a man accused of shaving his neighbor's show dog and then drawing a picture on the dog's back with permanent Magic Marker. What caused the matter to rise to the level of a felony was the subject of the drawing, which the defendant had rendered with the detail of a *Gray's Anatomy* illustration. Even the spectators who had been able to suppress guffaws when His Honor fell on the steps lost it when the factual basis for the dog-graffiti case was laid out. Weiner banged his gavel like a preschooler trying to drive the square block into the round hole and demanded that everyone "maintain the decorum required in court proceedings."

I had checked the schedule posted outside the courtroom when I first arrived, and my case was up next—a lucky position for an attorney on a schedule. The case was called, and I began to rise, but Weiner gestured for me to stay seated.

"We have a couple of related matters on the docket. As such, I will hold them until the end of the calendar."

A couple of related matters? My client was charged with possession. Did Weiner mean he had a passel of drug cases? Or was something else going on?

When Mike's case was pushed to the end of the calendar as well, I figured the prosecution must have decided to charge Deacon Davis for Nelsen's murder.

My client would not be brought over from the jail until his case was called. I decided to dash across the street to give him a heads-up, certain his case would not be called for another hour, minimum.

Deacon Davis was in the holding pen, the court administration's equivalent of being on deck, so I didn't have to wait for a deputy to fetch him from a cell. I made it through the security check unmolested and then went directly to the small, barred room where prisoners sat on long metal benches, waiting for their cases to be called. I found Deacon Davis and motioned for him to lean close into the bars so that we could have a modicum of privacy. Since we couldn't shake hands, we settled for single-arc finger waves. I whispered what had happened in court, curving my hands around my mouth to make a noise funnel. I watched his reaction carefully.

I recognized the look in his eyes immediately. I had seen it many times in my practice. It was the look of someone who has lost all hope of happy endings and for whom endurance trumps hope.

"Do you know of evidence, other than your fingerprints at the murder site, the prosecution could have?" I whispered urgently.

"What does it matter?" His tone was flat. He didn't bother to whisper.

I narrowed my eyes and placed my hands on my hips. "This is important. Do not for one second think of giving up. I've got a damn good track record in this business. Don't screw it up."

His eyes widened in surprise, but then a smile tugged at the corners of his mouth.

"Yes, ma'am." He pinched his eyes together and made a show of great concentration. Then his features relaxed slightly into a look of real concentration.

"What did Mr. Nelsen hang himself with?" he asked.

"I don't know yet. Since you haven't been charged in connection with the murder yet, I haven't been able to get a copy of the police report. Why?"

"Because I had a roll of twine I was usin' to tie shut garbage bags once they was full. One piece ain't strong enough to hold up a body, but if you double it up, it might work."

Could that have been it? Was it even possible to pull fingerprints off twine? DNA maybe, but they wouldn't have had time to run a full DNA analysis.

A deputy came over and tapped me on the shoulder.

"I'm sorry to interrupt, ma'am, but we have to take your client across the street. By the way, when Judge Weiner called the case and you weren't there, he threw a hissy fit. Just thought I'd warn you."

I had severely misjudged the time until our case was called, but I was used to Judge Weiner's hissy fits, so I wasn't too concerned. Still, I hightailed it back to his court before his bad humor escalated into a full-blown tantrum.

The fates were not with me. I ran into heavy pedestrian traffic on the way. I darted in and out to take advantage of gaps in the mass of humanity streaming across the street. I misjudged the capacity of one of those gaps and slammed into a man carrying a Coke and a hot dog piled high with condiments. I caught the hot dog before it hit the ground, but the Coke flew everywhere. Some of the condiments made a dash for freedom too, and my hand was coated with a muddy combination of mustard, ketchup, relish, and onions. I returned the hot dog to the man, muttered an attenuated apology, and raced up the courthouse steps, scrubbing my hands with a napkin I'd liberated from the hot-dog man.

As soon as I entered the courtroom, Judge Weiner went after his pound of flesh.

"Miss Williams, this is not one of your cocktail parties. You cannot be fashionably late here."

Cocktail parties? Seriously?

"No, Your Honor," I said contritely. "I apologize to the court."

He wasn't through, though.

"This court has a full schedule. I don't have time to wait while you run off to the ladies' room to fix your hair."

This was getting to be too much. "Your Honor, I was not—"

"What is that—hair mousse? I don't like it."

I automatically reached up to check my hair and felt something wet. I pulled my hand back, and it was covered with mustard.

A deputy escorted Deacon Davis in at that moment, and I was saved from having to explain my hot-dog collision.

I didn't have a Kleenex available, and the napkin was saturated, so I surreptitiously licked the mustard off my hand while Judge Weiner was distracted with Davis's entrance. Mike saw me, though, and rolled his tongue over his lips suggestively.

Prick.

Standing next to Mike was Nelsen's son, who was indeed the man I had seen at the Arcadia house earlier that week.

Judge Weiner cleared his throat and addressed the prosecutor. Tom Young had been replaced by a young female attorney who looked as if she were barely out of high school.

"Miss Hagarty, it is my understanding that the prosecution wishes to dismiss the charge of drug possession against Mr. Davis and has filed charges of murder and conspiracy to murder against both Mr. Davis and Mr. Nelsen, arising out of the same circumstances."

"Yes, Your Honor," Hagarty responded cheerfully.

"Your Honor, neither my client nor I have received a copy of the new charges. I respectively request time to review and discuss the new charges with my client," I said.

"You have fifteen minutes, Miss Williams," intoned Weiner.

"*Ms.,*" I said, but he pretended not to hear.

I pulled Deacon Davis into the hallway. "I'm asking again if there is anything you haven't told me that could tie you to the murder of Nelsen Nelsen."

"No. I told you everything I know. What's this about a conspiracy?"

I looked at the copy of the charges the prosecutor had handed me. "The state is alleging that you conspired with Mr. Nelsen Nelsen Jr.—Nelsen Nelsen's son—to murder Mr. Nelsen Sr."

"I never seen that guy until today," protested the deacon. "Either they got a video of me sleepwalkin', or they got nothin'."

I was pretty sure he was kidding about the sleepwalking, but I had to ask. "Do you sleepwalk?"

"I been married three times, and my wives complained about a lot of things, but sleepwalkin' wasn't one of 'em."

We returned to the courtroom, and I made the best argument I could for releasing Deacon Davis on a low bond, but Weiner didn't buy it. Deacon Davis and Nelsen Nelsen Jr.'s bonds were set at $100,000 each. I could tell from Nelsen Jr.'s reaction that he would have no trouble posting his bond.

I left Deacon Davis at the jail after reassuring him that my staff and I would pull out the stops and go above and beyond to get him out of there.

I called my office on the way back, and Beth, who sounded as if she were feeling better, answered. She said Sam and MJ were on phone calls, but Tuwanda had dropped by and was waiting in my office to take me to an early lunch, and she had mentioned something about a ghost hunt earlier that morning. Beth delivered this information with a heavy note of sarcasm.

Beth does not share Tuwanda and Venus's penchant for the occult.

I secretly enjoy forays into the otherworld, but today I'd had too much to do and had to skip that morning's event.

Tuwanda was sitting behind my desk, holding one of the heart-shaped pillows, when I walked in.

"You rentin' this place out for weddings and funerals now?" she asked, straight-faced.

"Very funny."

"I'm gonna ask your mom to decorate Walter's room. I think he'd really go for somethin' like this. Maybe change out the wide-eyed kid pictures for some wide-eyed dog pictures, but otherwise, it'd work fine."

I looked at her carefully to see if she was kidding, but she seemed serious.

Great. My office looks like a doghouse.

We rode together in Tuwanda's car, which looked like a parade float, to Paco's, a popular Mexican-food restaurant. Since it was early, we didn't have a problem finding a seat in the normally packed dining room.

After we ordered, I asked, "What happened at the ghost hunt?"

"It was a séance. 'Ghost hunt' sounds too much like that shit on TV. It went fine, and you'll be happy to know there's no ghosts in your house except for one that wandered over from the house across the street because she didn't like it there. But I got a great idea. We gonna have a séance at the bakery."

"What spirits do you expect to find at the bakery?"

"Nelsen, of course, plus lots of witnesses. Din't you say it was bein' used as a drug house? People die cuz of drugs all the time. I bet there's a whole mess of spirits sittin' around with nothin' better to do than watch the goin's-on in the buildin'."

"So you're suggesting we give Venus a call and set something up?"

Tuwanda shook her head and looked at me earnestly. "I can do it. I know I can, Katie. I've seen Venus do it tons of times, and it ain't that hard."

"But you haven't seen or heard any of the spirits Venus contacts. How will you know if one is talking to you?"

"Simple. I'll be the one communicatin' with 'em this time, not Venus. I just gotta get 'em to focus on me."

This bizarre conversation was interrupted when the waitress came with our food. (One of the things I love about Mexican food is the short prep time. It's the James Mulvihill of fast foods.)

Tuwanda picked up on the subject again as soon as the waitress left.

"You said yourself yesterday that this is a tough case because there ain't no witnesses."

I didn't remember saying that, but it was true.

I took a bite of a bean burrito the size of a sleeping bag and wiped cheese off my chin. "You have a point, but I don't have time to talk to spirits. I have to exhaust traditional avenues of investigation first, and Sam, MJ, and I have just started."

"So we'll do it in your off-hours."

"Attorneys don't have off-hours," I stated resignedly. "At least when you have a client sitting in the Fourth Avenue jail charged with murder."

"That place is nasty," commented Tuwanda with feeling. "Let's say we do this then: if you can't find no more livin' witnesses before tonight, we'll go to the old bakery and find us some dead ones."

I opened my mouth to protest, but she held her hand up. "I know what you're gonna say: spirits can't testify at trial. But they *can* give you information that'll help your investigation."

Figuring I had nothing to lose, I agreed with Tuwanda's plan and said I would call at five o'clock to confirm whether our ghost hunt was on. I figured Sam, MJ, and I would have a live lead by then, and I could in good conscience cancel the ghost hunt.

CHAPTER 9

I was wrong. By late afternoon, we had reviewed the police reports and interviewed Deacon Washington.

The police reports and charging documents outlined a case against Davis that relied on Nelsen Jr.'s admission that he had been at the bakery earlier with his father to "discuss financial issues." According to the prosecutor's version of events, Deacon Davis had been hired by Nelsen Jr. to kill Nelsen Sr. and had either been in the building when the Nelsens were there or arrived soon after Nelsen Jr.'s departure.

Davis's DNA matched that found on the twine around Nelsen's neck.

Deacon Washington verified what Davis had told me, but he could add nothing new. Sam hadn't been able to unearth any more witnesses, so we had little evidence on our side. The good part—if you could call it that—was that the prosecution didn't have much evidence either.

I looked at the clock. It was already five. I decided that since I had no other plans for the evening—other than work, which was always available for a good time—I might as well go to Tuwanda's bakery séance. I didn't seriously think Tuwanda was going to conjure up any helpful spirits—or any spirits at all, for that matter—but I was curious to see the crime site. It always helps me in my case preparation if I've seen where the alleged crime happened.

I caught Tuwanda as she was about to leave and go conjuring solo. She agreed to swing by my office to pick me up.

I invited Sam and MJ to come with us, but both gave me the rolling-eyes treatment and cautioned me about sneaking around South Phoenix at night. Sam even went so far as to give me one of his guns—a nifty little .38 with a pearl handle. I took it from him to make him happy but had no intention of using it. I shot someone once and don't plan on repeating the experience.

I shoved the gun into a desk drawer as soon as Sam and MJ left.

Tuwanda's '83 Cadillac was not out of place in South Phoenix since all the cars we saw were at least twenty years old. We parked a block from the bakery in an empty lot. Tuwanda took a flashlight out of the trunk, and I made sure I had my cell phone. Tuwanda had forgotten hers.

The heat was less intense in the fading sunlight, and the short walk to the old bakery was almost pleasant. As had been the case on my last visit, the sound of swamp coolers drowned out all other noises.

The crime-scene tape was gone, which made our entry less illegal. (We were not disturbing a crime scene, but we were still trespassing.) The building looked as derelict as I remembered, but it now had a sinister air about it due to its association with murder.

A plastic grocery bag borne on a slight breeze floated across our path. I heard a sudden intake of breath as Tuwanda stopped short and grabbed my arm.

"Your first ghost," I joked.

"You stop that. We gotta be on the alert for all signs of the paranormal. I'm just bein' diligent."

I headed for the window with the loose chicken wire, assuming that the police had locked the front door before they left. Taking a deep breath, I peeled the wire back and entered the same way Lonny had, minus the extra propulsion afforded by Officer Bridges's foot. When I landed inside headfirst, I reacted the same way Lonnie had.

"Gross!" I yelled.

Tuwanda opened the front door and walked in.

"What the hell you doin'?" she asked, sweeping her flashlight's beam around the room. "That floor's nasty. Oh my Lord, is that what I think it is?" She focused the light on a Slurpee cup filled with used condoms sitting next to an old mattress.

"Man, I am spending way too much on overhead," she muttered.

"Gross," I repeated. I stood and dusted my hands on my pants, silently apologizing to Michael Kors.

The room we were standing in was huge—a story and a half high and the size of a ballroom. This was where the guts of the bakery had been. A cold room stood in the back corner, its insulated door hanging on one hinge. An old conveyor belt was all that was left of the equipment. The rest had probably been taken by either the bakery's creditors or ambitious thieves.

"Nelsen was murdered on the third floor," I said, pointing to metal stairs zigzagging up the wall at the back of the room.

Tuwanda took the lead, shining her flashlight in front of us and describing items of detritus we encountered along the way.

"Looka that: the front page of a newspaper announcin' the bombin' of the Twin Towers. An' there's a copy of *People* with Mel Gibson on the front, an' they ain't sayin' anythin' bad about him. Things sure has changed."

The building was like a time capsule covering the last twenty-five years. I'd forgotten how much September 11, 2001, had changed things. Everything published before that memorable date seemed naive when viewed through post-September 11 glasses. The bars for fear and paranoia were set low these days.

The tiny second floor looked as if it had been used for storage. The third floor consisted of a rabbit warren of offices, some still holding dusty plastic chairs and metal desks. The third floor was noticeably cleaner than the lower floors, probably due to Deacon Davis and Deacon Washington's cleaning and the evidence-collection efforts of the Phoenix PD.

We located the room where Nelsen's body had been found. White police tape on the linoleum floor indicated the place over which the body had hung. Several acoustic ceiling tiles had been removed to expose a white-taped portion of a steel pipe. I didn't see any twine, but a stack of garbage bags still lay in the corner. I took a picture of it with my cell-phone camera.

Tuwanda, who was standing by the window, started chanting something under her breath.

"Venus doesn't chant," I pointed out.

"Each medium's got they own secret tricks for contactin' the departed. Mine's chantin'."

"What are you chanting?"

"If I tol' you, it wouldn't be secret. Now, quit interruptin'."

I strained to hear, and as best as I could tell, Tuwanda's special chant sounded a lot like the Black Eyed Peas' "Let's Get It Started."

I began humming along, but we were barely into the refrain when a bright light coming from outside flashed through the window. I joined Tuwanda in searching for the source of the light.

"It's one of the spirits," whispered Tuwanda excitedly.

"It was probably a car headlight," I scoffed. It was strange, though, because headlights don't usually flash through third-story windows, cars being land-bound and all.

We heard a low whir and saw another flash of light. Splinters and sparks flew from the window frame. A quarter-sized hole appeared on the frame.

"Spirits don't use weapons," I said tersely, pulling Tuwanda away from the window.

"Maybe around here they do. It's pro'bly jus' as dangerous here for spirits as it is for people."

We heard the front door crash open.

"Shhh," I commanded.

Footsteps sounded on the stairs.

The police.

I dragged Tuwanda to a window on the other side of the building and tore back the chicken wire.

"Go out the window," I said urgently.

"An' do what? Fall? Gravity's one of the few things that still works in South Phoenix."

"No. I'll boost you up to the roof. Then you can pull me up. Hurry. Now!"

Tuwanda placed her flashlight on the floor and climbed onto the windowsill. I held her ankles while she reached up and grabbed the top edge of the parapet surrounding the flat roof. Then I crouched down, braced my shoulder against the wall, and lifted. Every muscle and tendon in my body screamed in protest, but I boosted Tuwanda high enough for her to pull herself over the parapet and onto the roof.

Just as her feet disappeared, another flash of light lit up the yard.

CHAPTER 10

TUWANDA

Katie was reachin' up to me, and then—*poof*—she was gone. I stayed where I was, listenin', but I din't hear nothin'. I listened to nothin' for a while longer. On the one hand, quiet was a good sign because I knew Katie would make noise she was hurt or in trouble. On the other hand, she might be hurt so bad that she couldn't talk. The thought of her bein' in trouble was what made me go back down into that buildin' even though I was so scared I was shakin'.

Since shakin' interferes with climbin' over a wall and swingin' into a window, I figured I'd better find a route that involved less Tarzan shit. I felt my way over that dirty, littered roof, grateful that I couldn't see nothin', because not seein' kept me from knowin' what I was touchin'.

On my third pass over the roof, I felt the outline of a trapdoor and, even better, found a metal ring in the middle of it. I pulled on the ring, and it didn't budge. I pulled and pulled, feelin' like them losers who couldn't pull the sword out of the stone before Arthur eased it out like it was nothin'.

Finally, the door made a grating noise and swung open. I waited and listened to make sure none of the bad guys had heard anything, and then I looked down into the opening.

Phoenix don't have moonlight or starlight, but we do have lots of light pollution, so I could make out the outline of the top rung of a metal ladder. I rolled onto my stomach with my legs hanging though the trapdoor. I felt around with my feet until my right foot landed on a ladder rung. After that, it was easy.

I climbed down into a small room I hadn't seen when Katie and me looked around before. The room where Nelsen died was a fair-sized office. This one was more along the lines of a large closet. I tripped over something lying on the floor, and by touch, I identified it as a broom. I figured I was probably in a janitor's closet or a utility room.

I held that broom in front of me, it bein' the closest thing I had to a weapon, and ran my hand along the walls, lookin' for a door. Boxes were piled up against the walls and stacked in the middle, though, and I knocked a bunch of 'em down when I ricocheted off a metal desk after my knee bounced off a chair. I gave the broom a shake because it wasn't bein' much help at all.

Papers spilled out of the fallen boxes. I felt a raised panel on the wall where they'd been piled. By the size of it, I guessed it was an electrical-panel cover, and it was padlocked shut. I guess the owner din't want no one to mess around with the electric, though it din't make no difference now, because the power pro'bly hadn't been on for years.

I shoved some more boxes on the floor and felt what I thought was a cupboard door. Most likely, it opened up on storage shelves, because it had one of them pulls instead of a knob and was shorter than most doors. I pushed on the door, an' nothin' happened. Then I pushed it hard, more out of frustration than anything else. The door slid open. Outside was a hallway that led to where Nelsen had died. I could tell by the window and police tape.

I searched that hall and the room like a junkie lookin' for a fix, but there wasn't no sign of Katie. There wasn't no sign of anyone else bein' there either. Everythin' looked jus' the way Katie an' me first seen it.

I searched the second and first floors, too, but didn't find no sign of anyone there either.

When I got outside, I walked to the first house I came to with its lights on and knocked on the door.

"Who's there?" It was a man's voice, all low and growly— the kinda voice people use when they's holdin' a baseball bat.

Welcome back to the neighborhood.

"My name's Tuwanda, an' I need to use your phone to report a missin' person."

The door opened a crack, and a reddened eye gave me the once-over. "Ebhoni's kid?"

"Who's askin'?"

"The one whose phone you want to use."

He opened the door wider, and I seen this tall, skinny guy with gray hair and black-as-coal skin.

"Roderick? Roderick Wilmont?"

"Yep. What brings you to South Phoenix, Tuwanda? I thought you got out of here and never looked back. Don't tell me the economy's got to you too, and you're havin' to go door to door to drum up business."

I didn't take no offense. South Phoenicians understand survival, and they don't look down they noses at any kind of work.

"Roderick, I got an emergency on my hands, an' I need to use your phone. I was over at that ole bakery buildin', an'—"

"Oh no—that place? Tell me you ain't sunk that low."

I ignored him and plowed on.

"You live a couple houses away. Did you see them bright lights over there?"

"Yeah, we seen 'em. We seein' lights over there all the time. A couple junkies even burned themselves up in there last year. When we seen the lights tonight, we figured it was the cops takin' more pictures because of the murder. Maybe you ain't heard yet, but the guy that run the bakery back in the day got killed in there. You pro'bly don't remember him, cuz you was too busy tryin' to keep your mom off the street wearin' that crazy white makeup of hers. But he used to employ a lot of people in this neighborhood."

"Roderick, I need to use your phone," I said, bringin' Roderick back to the point.

"Well, hell, girl. Why didn't you say so? Come on in. It's in the kitchen."

Since the livin' room and the kitchen was one big room, I din't have no problem findin' my way. The house smelled like decades of cookin' odors, and the room, though it was tidy enough, was crowded with furniture and knickknacks that showed someone in the house was a big baseball fan. I picked up the phone, but as soon as I dialed 911, Roderick snatched it out of my hand.

"What the hell you doin', girl? Ain't nobody callin' the police on this phone. I don't want nothin' to do with Phoenix's finest."

"My friend's missin'. There was this big flash of blue light and—*poof*—she was gone."

"Maybe she just wandered off."

"It's not like Katie to do that. She wouldn't leave without tellin' me."

"Tell you what: let's you and me take a look around, and if we don't find her all safe and sound after a half hour, then we'll call the police. You make sure to tell 'em, though, that I got nothin' to do with any of this. I'm an innocent bystander. Hell, I ain't even that much. I just answered the damn door."

I knew I wasn't gonna get nowhere with Roderick. Soon as the folks down here hear the word *police*, they turn into them monkeys that don't see, hear, or say nothin'. I don' blame 'em, cuz anything they say can and will be held against 'em.

"Let's get goin' then. You got a mobile phone, Roderick?"

He nodded.

"Then bring it in case we need to call for help."

"Okay, but 'member, I don't—"

"You don't got nothin' to do with nothin'," I finished for him. "I get it. You make a lousy Good Samaritan, Roderick—you know that?"

"The Good Samaritan din't have to deal with no Phoenix police."

Roderick grabbed a couple flashlights and a Nokia phone from the kitchen counter, and we stepped out onto the porch. I kept walkin', but he paused to triple lock the door before catchin' up with me. He handed me the smaller of the two flashlights.

I motioned toward the old bakery. "We'll check aroun' the buildin' first and then search west to Twenty-Fourth and north to Broadway."

Roderick fell into step beside me.

"What's your friend look like?" he asked.

Tears welled up as I pictured Kate, and I had to clear my throat before I could talk. "She's about five feet eight, blondish hair, got a real nice figure and a pretty face, although you can't tell her that. She got low self-esteem. I met her mom a couple days ago, an' I can see why. That woman could make Jesus Christ hisself feel like a failure."

Roderick cleared his throat softly.

"Too much information?" I asked. "I guess I'm just nervous."

"Actually, you leavin' out a big piece of information. Is this friend of yours white?"

"She is, but she's one of them white people where you forget what color they is after a while because it don't make no difference to her, and so it don't make no difference to you."

"It makes a difference in this neighborhood. People'd notice a white woman wanderin' around at this time of night. If she's around, someone musta noticed."

We separated in front of the bakery, with Roderick takin' one side of the building and me the other. It took me longer because my light wasn't as strong as Roderick's, an' I wasn't goin' to let no weak light get in the way of serious searchin'. I moved slow, bein' careful not to miss anythin'.

I waded through knee-high weeds and stepped over pieces of rusted shit that din't look like they was ever anythin' useful. I saw Roderick waitin' for me when I rounded the corner. At the same time, I saw, way back near the rear fence, an empty Cheetos bag that was glowin' green. I headed for the Cheetos bag, callin' for Roderick to follow me. I lost sight of the bag a couple of times due to obstructin' pieces of garbage but finally got to where it was.

I bent down to get a closer look. I ain't a nervous person by nature, but with my state of mind bein' what it was, I was half expectin' to find a hunk of Kryptonite. It wasn't, though. It was Katie's cell phone.

Using a piece of Kleenex in case of fingerprint evidence, I picked it up and stared at the screen. Katie had typed 9-1 and didn't get no further. That was enough for me.

"We gotta call the police, Roderick. She's in trouble."

He sighed and reluctantly handed me his phone.

The 911 operator was some young new thing who musta topped her procedures class but wasn't payin' attention during the half-hour session on public relations.

"Your name, please," she said, sounding snippy, like I was interruptin' somethin' way more important.

"Tuwanda Jones. Listen, my friend up and disappeared in a flash of light. I'm scared she's hurt."

"Is that Tuwanda with a *T* or with a *D?*"

"It's Tuwanda with a lawsuit headin' your way if you don't speed things up."

"Where are you calling from, ma'am?"

"I'm standin' in a nasty field in back of an old bakery at about Twentieth Street and Yucca."

"Are you in a secure location, ma'am?"

"Hell no."

"Please calmly and succinctly state the reason for your call."

"You know, don't you, that folks callin' 911 ain't at all calm, and most don't know what succinct means? Lucky for you, I do."

"Do your best, ma'am."

"As I was sayin', there was this big flash of light, and my friend disappeared. I went to get help from a nearby homeowner—"

"Actually, I rent," whispered Roderick.

"Who said he'd help me look for her. We jus' found her cell phone lyin' in a field behind the bakery buildin'. It looks like she dialed nine and one but got … interrupted before she could finish." I din't want to think about how Kate got interrupted.

"Please describe the nature of the flash of light, ma'am."

"It was a bright blue light. My friend was on the third floor of the buildin' when it happened, and I was on the roof. I searched the buildin', but she was just gone."

"Have you been drinking alcohol or taking anything that might alter your perception of reality, ma'am?"

"No. Why ain't you tellin' the dispatcher to send someone out here?"

"Do you have authority to grant the police permission to enter the building premises?"

"No, but there's exigent circumstances here. So you don't need no permission or a warrant."

In my kind of bidness, you gotta know that Fourth Amendment shit.

"Ma'am, I will notify a patrol car in your area of the circumstances, but a flash of blue light is not an emergency condition requiring immediate dispatch of officers. If you would like, I can transfer you to our missing-persons department, and you can file a report with them."

"Is your supervisor around?"

"Yes, ma'am, but I don't think—"

"Do me a favor and tell him or her that you got a 911 call on the disappearance of Caitlin Williams, Esquire."

"Williams? I've heard of her."

"Damn right you have."

Within seconds, another voice came on the line. "What's this about Kate missing?"

"Hi, this here's Tuwanda Jones, and we got a situation here. Katie's gone missin' in South Phoenix, an'—"

"We'll send a car out."

And that was that.

"Is they on the way?" asked Roderick, taking his phone back.

"Yes, sir."

"Then I am out of the way. Just drop the flashlight off in my mailbox when you're done."

He disappeared into the night, an' I walked around to the front of the buildin' so the police could spot me.

I din't want to sit down, for fear of gettin' tetanus or syphilis or God knows what else, so I found a cleanish spot and planted myself on it. Not havin' much else to do, I punched the buttons on Kate's phone and checked her e-mails (she had an e-mail from Jane about a house inspection), her texts (she had one from Jane about the house inspection and another one from Beth, telling her Jane had called about a house inspection), and her photos. There were some real cute pictures of Ralph and a picture of Bryan that if the newspapers got their hands on it, would either make or destroy his career, dependin' on the demographic. The las' photo looked like it was taken by mistake. I did that a lot. I got a big collection of floor-tile photos.

The photo was too dark to see much of anything, except … *What the hell?* If you looked real close, you could see the outline of a something with either eight arms or seven arms and a head. One arm bein' shorter and thicker than the others, it was hard to tell. It was standin' in a doorway, dressed in a long light-colored robe that hung to the floor. I looked at the date of the photo, thinkin' it might be an old Halloween picture or was from one of Sam's weird costume parties. But the date was today, and the time was an hour ago.

I'm norm'ly a calm woman, but this pushed the calm right out of me. I swung my flashlight around. For all I knew, I could be standin' in the middle of one of them crop circles.

Lookin' back on it now, I don' know why alien agricultural practices scare anyone, but when you're alone in a dark, strange place, these things are of concern.

While I was considerin' whether a burned-out spot in the grass was the remains of a campfire or the landin' site of a UFO, I caught sight of headlights bouncin' down the road toward the bakery. The scraping sound every time that patrol car bottomed out in a pothole was gratifyin'. The city might give serious consideration to pavin' the roads down here next time the issue come up.

The car slowed to a stop, and two men got out. One was in uniform; the other was in plain clothes. Actually, since the ununiformed guy was Webber, *plain clothes* ain't the right term. *Loud and tacky* fits better.

"What's going on here, Tuwanda?" asked Webber impatiently and kinda rude, like I'd interrupted his favorite TV show.

"Whatsa matter? You had to leave before Big Bird gave the word of the day?"

"Can it, Tuwanda. What happened to Kate?"

The tears came, and I couldn't stop 'em. "I don't know," I burbled. I got a grip and hiccupped and sniffed my way through the story from beginning to end.

"You were here looking for ghosts, and you think she got abducted by an alien?"

"It don't sound so good when you say it," I snuffled.

Another cop car and an evidence van bounced down the road and pulled up behind the first cop car.

Webber waved his hands at them in a go-back motion and said, "False alarm, guys,"

"Wait a minute, Webber. Take a look at this here photo on Kate's phone. It's the last one she took before she disappeared."

Webber took Kate's phone and squinted at the picture. "That's probably Sam dressed up for one of his queer-guy costume parties."

"No, it ain't. Look at the time it was taken."

He paused to stare at it intently but still wasn't convinced. "This is just a joke someone's playing on you and Kate."

"Who the hell would be playin' a joke like that? It ain't at all funny. Plus, jokers don't, as a rule, *shoot* at the jokees."

"Shoot? You didn't say anything about a shooting. When? Where?"

"Well, it wasn't so much a shootin' as it was a zappin'. I'll show you."

Webber motioned for the evidence-collection guys to follow. I took 'em up to the third floor and showed them the windowsill. One of the evidence guys, who introduced himself as Officer Walchik, shined a bright light where I pointed, and the other officer took pictures from diff'rent angles, kinda like one of them fashion photographers, except he wasn't tellin' anyone to toss their hair or look flirty. When he was done takin' pictures, he handed his camera to Webber, examined the charring, and then scraped the damaged parts into a baggy. Webber, Walchik, and me watched like we was witnessin' the Second Comin'. None of us so much as breathed.

"What do you think?" Webber whispered once the scraping was done.

"Laser," the scraper officer said. "Strong one. There's gonna be more holes along the laser's trajectory."

Sure enough, there was a round hole higher up on the opposite wall.

"What do you mean by that?" asked Webber, droppin' the whisper and goin' back to his normal, finger-nails-on-blackboard voice.

The scraper officer straightened and took a deep breath. He had one of them serious but excited looks that you know means the topic about to be addressed ain't just one about which he's got superior knowledge. It's an obsession.

The crazy-eyed laser guy gave us a lecture on lasers. I'm a well-educated woman—I got fifteen credits at the community college toward a degree in psychology—but most of what this guy said was way over my head. My thinkin' is that I don't care how much you know—if people don't understan' what you sayin' or it's too damn boring to keep their int'rest, all that knowledge don't mean crap. If Moses come down from the mountain with a bunch of commandments that read like the instructions for a DVD player, we'd still be worshippin' a gold calf.

After ten minutes, the laser guy showed no signs of slowin' down. Instead of lettin' the lecture run its course, Webber, whose throat clearin' and nose scratchin' had picked up speed, finally couldn't take no more and interrupted him.

"Set up the lights, and search the area," he ordered.

The laser man looked disappointed at not bein' able to finish his speech, but he an' Officer Walchik followed orders.

They an' the other cops started settin' up a perimeter and doin' their other cop thing. Webber tol' me to sit in the backseat of a cop car and stay put. I borrowed Webber's phone—he'd taken Kate's and bagged it for evidence—and started makin' calls. I called Bryan, Beth, MJ, and Sam, and I didn't get none of the disbelief I got from Webber and his boys, because they know Kate and an alien abduction ain't all that impossible in Kate's world.

CHAPTER 11

WEBBER

I shouldn't have responded to the call on Williams. South Phoenix isn't even part of my assigned area. But no one else on the force has my kind of experience with the messes she gets into. That woman never saw a windmill she wouldn't fight or met a lost cause she wouldn't champion. The more you tell her to back off, the harder she goes at it.

I'd never tell her to her face, but her instincts and conclusions are good once you get by all the weirdness of her reasoning. Another thing I'd never tell her to her face is that I respect and like Kate. She comes through for people.

I was willing to give Tuwanda the benefit of the doubt, but when I heard the disappearing-into-a-flash-of-blue-light stuff, I was ready to call it off and find another hobby. The fact that the information came from Tuwanda didn't help. Tuwanda and I have a natural antagonism due to her running an illegal operation and my being an upstanding officer of the law. The only reason I tolerate her is that she's helped us out a couple of times. Plus, Kate likes her, and that counts for something.

What turned things around was the charred and splintered window frame. Johnson is a closet Trekkie and goes on and on when it comes to his subject, but I got the drift. That damage was caused by a weapons-grade laser. The navy tested a laser weapon in 2011 that took out a cruiser ten miles away. It was that kind of laser, not the kind used to point out shit on a diagram.

The laser was good news because not every Tom, Dick, and Harry could get their hands on something like that. He or she had to be someone connected with the military or government-funded R&D.

The first thing I did was call Colonel Richard Jeffries, the commander of Luke Air Force Base, who happens to be my brother-in-law. Dick—he hates it when I call him that—has no sense of humor. Other than that, he's a decent guy.

I figured he'd be at home, watching *NCIS*, and I was right. When his wife, Dee Dee, answered the phone, I could hear the opening music in the background. Then I heard a muffled exchange between Dee Dee and Dick. Dee Dee sounded pleasant at first, and Dick sounded annoyed; then Dee Dee's voice got low and ominous. A second later, Dick was on the phone.

"What is it, Fred?"

I explained what Johnson had said about the laser. Dick swore and hung up.

A half hour later, so many helicopters were overhead that it looked like the filming of *Independence Day*. I half-expected ninjas to slide down on ropes, but the birds landed one by one in the field. I wish my guys could make an entrance like that once in a while.

The first man to jump out was a disappointment. He was wearing a raincoat in what was still a hundred-degree heat. I could see his pajama bottoms underneath. It was Dick.

He got within an inch of my face and hissed, "What you told me had better be true. I don't want you making a fool out of me."

Yeah. God forbid it should turn out to be a hoax and the country is safe after all.

He was so close to me now that I could smell the Ovaltine on his breath.

I called Johnson over and asked him to escort the colonel and his men to the third-story window. I could tell by the look in Johnson's eyes that this was the most exciting thing that had happened in his life and knew Dick and his guys were in for a two-hour lecture unless they got Johnson under control early on.

All in all, despite the crowd of police and military, things were organized and proceeding smoothly. But I'd forgotten about the wild card.

Tuwanda was sitting in one of the patrol cars, waiting for an officer to interview her. As soon as Dick and his men disappeared into the old bakery, she got out and headed in my direction.

She said, "This is cool and shit with all them GI Joes flyin' in and givin' Johnson a hard-on and all, but I don't see no one lookin for Kate. That bein' the case, I'm gonna leave and do some of my own investigatin'. If you want me, you can call me on my cell phone."

With that, she turned on her heel and walked away.

"You have not been released yet," I said. "We do not have your statement." I gave it the old college try, but it sounded lame even to me. Tuwanda and I both knew I wasn't about to put her in custody, and short of that, there wasn't much I could do.

I watched her out of the corner of my eye and was surprised when she walked to a dilapidated little white house instead of to her car. She knocked on the door, and a hand snaked out, grabbed her by her wrist, and pulled her inside. I wrote down the address and asked one of my guys to run a records check on it. The house's resident was likely a friend of hers from the old days in South Phoenix, but I wanted to make sure.

CHAPTER 12

TUWANDA

Roderick wasn't real pleased to see me. I think he figured he'd done his civic duty for this lifetime and there wasn't anythin' left owed until he came back in his next life as a rabbit or a coyote or some other shit like that.

I told him what I wanted him to do.

"Uh-uh, girl. Like I said, I'd be happy to help out an old friend from the neighborhood so long as in doin' so, I don't gotta deal with no cops. I'm gonna go ahead and update that avoidance rule to include soldiers, too. What the hell is this all about anyways? Now that they pullin' out of Iraq and Afghanistan, they goin' after South Phoenix?"

"They just overreactin' to some ash on a windowsill they say was caused by a special kinda weapon."

"You kiddin', right? My fifteen-year-old nephew's got something that can flatten a buildin' in one shot, and my government is worryin' about a charred window frame? Damn. It's still a white man's world. Ain't no black man that'd ever act that way."

"Now that you vented your feelin's, you gonna help me or not?"

"Weren't you listenin', girl? No way am I gonna—"

I gave him the Tuwanda face, and he hesitated. I learned the basic expression of disgust from my mom and then embellished it with other emotions as I grew up. I believe it's about perfected now: a combination of disdain, anger, disappointment, and, of course, disgust. I once asked Kate about copywritin' it, but she said it wasn't necessary since it's unlikely anyone else could duplicate it.

"All right, girl. I'll help you. But I can't be stayin up all night with this shit. I got to go to work in the mornin'."

"You don't got no job."

"Lookin' for a job *is* a job."

"No arguin' with that. Let's get goin then. We gotta go house to house and find out if anyone saw anythin'."

At each house I went to, I got the same "I'm holdin' a baseball bat—what you want?" greeting. After we got through the traditional ghetto opening ceremonies where both sides establish their hood creds, I had to listen to reminiscences about my weird mom.

No one had much new to add about the goin's-on at the bakery. In fact, I was givin' out more information than I was gettin', cuz everyone had questions 'bout the helicopters. I hoped Roderick was doin' better than me.

I came to a house set back from the road, behind a chain-link fence. A gate barely hangin' on by one hinge din't do much to help the Keep Out sign make the point. The front of the house was dark, but I could see a light in the back, an' the yard was lit by the kinda bright light you see in prison yards.

Lots of times, you see a house in South Phoenix that barely looks big enough for one person, and it turns out it's a duplex or even a triplex. Although it was the size of a single garage, this one had one apartment in the back and one in front.

Through a side window, I thought I saw a backlit child-sized person movin' aroun'. In this neighborhood, that meant a kid or kids were home alone and instructed by a parent workin' the night shift to never open the door to no one! Judgin' by the size of the shadow I seen, I'm guessin' it was a nine- or ten-year-old. That's old enough to load and fire down here, so I knew to be careful.

I went around to the back of the house, walkin' over bare dirt littered with plastic grocery bags, empty prescription and beer bottles, an' McDonald's wrappers—standard landscapin' in South Phoenix. I knocked on the door.

The shadow inside froze.

I knocked again and this time called out, "Don' be afraid. I jus' want to know if anyone seen anythin' weird goin' on at the old bakery over the last coupla days."

There was still no answer. I thought maybe I should be more specific. "I mean like if anyone seen somethin' like a spaceship or aliens, not the usual weird. We raisin' the bar here."

I was about to turn away, figurin' the shadow I seen was maybe a dog so big he din't have to bark to get the point across, when I hear this little voice.

"You payin' for information?"

I just 'bout got misty-eyed thinkin' about the sweet innocence of youth.

"I'll pay what it's worth. If I don' think it's worth anythin', you don't get nothin'."

"Seems pretty one-sided. I think I need somethin' up front, cuz once it's out of my mouth, I lose my lev'rage. My mom say you get nothin' in life without lev'rage, whether it's made up or not."

His mom was a wise woman, and she din't raise no fool.

Normally, I'd negotiate harder, but I was in a hurry. "I'm gonna slip a dollar bill under the door as a down payment. If what you tell me is helpful, then I'm gonna slip another dollar under the door."

I reached down, shoved a dollar under the door, and then waited. I could see the kid checking the money to make sure it was real.

"Let's keep this movin', junior," I prompted.

"It's Jevon, not junior. I maybe seen a shiny dude with lots of arms hangin' around the bakery the last coupla days."

"What you mean you *maybe* seen? Seems like a shiny person with lots of arms is somethin' you see or don't see. Ain't no maybe about it."

He didn't say nothin, so I shoved another dollar under the door.

"Wasn't no maybe about it, but when I told my mom, she smacked me on the butt, and I'm findin' that sayin *maybe* saves my butt."

"So did you see where this person with all the arms come from?"

"Do you mean like did he get out of a spaceship? Uh-uh. I din't see no spaceship. All I saw was a Jeep Cherokee. I guess if you got all them arms, you don't want to bring more attention to yourself by drivin' a spaceship around. Hey, do you think that Jeep was a spaceship disguised to look like a Jeep?"

We was gettin' off topic.

"Was this guy goin' in or comin' out of the bakery or jus' hangin' around outside?"

"He was goin in *and* out, like he was lookin' for somethin'. That was the day before yesterday, 'bout three. When I seen him about five this afternoon, he was creepin' around in back of the buildin'. Then I seen—"

"Was he carryin' anythin'?" I was gettin' excited now. If what Jevon said was true, it meant the octopus man was already there when Kate an' me got to the buildin'. Plus, he may have been there when Nelsen got hanged.

"Don't know if he had anything in his hands. When a man's got a bunch of arms, it's hard to see what all of 'em's doin'. Besides, you're fixed on why he got so many arms, and you ain't noticin' anything else."

Jevon not seein' the octopus man carryin' a laser didn't dampen my excitement. Hell, I don't even know what a laser looks like, and Jevon probably din't either. Could be one of the octopus man's arms had laser powers. You can't limit your thinkin' when it comes to aliens.

"Did you watch him leave? Was he alone?"

"The first day I seen him, I din't stick around to see him leave, on account of my momma screamin' for me to come home. Earlier today, when I seen him again, the alien came runnin' out of the bakery and hid out in back. Then a couple ladies walked up and started lookin' around. They didn't look like church people, cops, or junkies. They looked more businesslike. Soon as they come up, though, my momma called me to come home. Cell phones don't do nothin' 'cept extend the distance my momma can yell.

"I was mad later on, when all them helicopters showed up and I'd missed whatever happened. I figured them two ladies must o' run into Jelly Man and called the Men in Black or somethin'."

"Why you call him Jelly Man? You said he was shiny."

"Yeah. Like how Vaseline's shiny. I know cuz my momma put that stuff on everything: furniture, door hinges, people. This guy looked like he had about three inches of Vaseline on, an' you could see his innards underneath."

I revised my mental image from Reynolds Wrap to aspic, which I had once at a weddin' an' thought tasted awful— might as well eat a spoonful of salt.

At first, I wanted to find Webber right away an' let him know what Jevon said, but then I had second thoughts. Webber don't trust me, cuz he considers me a criminal even after all the good me an' Kate have done catchin' bad guys that he and his men were too stupid an' lazy to find. I din't think Webber was gonna find the testimony of a nine- or ten-year-old—

"Jevon, how old are you?"

"Nine."

I didn't think the testimony of a nine-year-old kid about an eight-armed Vaseline man was gonna be persuasive.

CHAPTER 13

TUWANDA

I thanked Jevon and walked back out to the street before callin' Sam. After I tol' him what was goin' on and we agreed the police and soldiers weren't givin' Kate's disappearance proper attention, he tol' me he'd get MJ an' a few others, an' they'd come out and help me do the necessary investigatin'. I was grateful for the offer. Even with Roderick's help, it would take me all night to search the rest of the neighborhood door to door.

I gave Sam Roderick's address, and he promised they'd be there in under an hour.

Roderick was already at the house when I got there, and we sat out on the front steps, talkin' while we waited for Sam and his crew. Roderick said he din't have no luck findin' anyone who saw anythin' helpful, but I doubted he'd tried. He said he knew Jevon, though, an' that he was a good kid—just a little defensive about bein' small for his age.

The first of Sam and his arm to show up was Sam hisself, with MJ and her Harley hard on his tail. Sam parked his precious Volvo far enough away from the other vehicles to protect it from injury and dust. I could see he'd been at one of his costume parties and was still wearin' his Cher getup. MJ braked her pink Harley hard right next to the Volvo, sendin' a mist of dust over that overprotected Swedish princess.

Webber and his guys were too busy to notice they'd arrived. Some of the soldiers looked up, and you could tell they was trying not to laugh. Sam looks pretty good in his long-hair wig an' shimmery evenin' gown, but MJ was wearin' a black leather miniskirt that about showed everythin' since skirts aren't made for straddlin' bikes. She'd squeezed her bosom into a low-cut T-shirt that said *Dairy Free* on it.

I guess the soldiers only cared about findin' the laser, though, because they went back to searchin' as soon as they got all their giggles out.

Beth's little MINI Cooper came next. Beth, Venus, Ralph, and Larry, Kate's homeless son, piled out as soon as the car's motor was off. All of them except Ralph stood blinkin' in the harsh lights the police had set up, trying to take in the scene. Ralph trotted up to me and, dispensing with formalities, sniffed me to see if I been anywhere interesting lately.

Then Marge, my administrative assistant, drove up with a car full of Care Bares. I counted five of 'em.

The big surprise was the last group of searchers to arrive. Jane's BMW pulled up, an' she an' three other people, all wearin' business suits and their Happy Homes Realty badges, got out an' marched in unison over to where the rest of us was standin'.

That woman wasn't goin' to let go of a commission without a fight. I almost felt sorry for the alien.

The last passenger emergin' from the backseat of Jane's car was Kate's mom. She straightened her skirt and looked around distasteful-like. If you ask my opinion, she looked more inconvenienced than concerned.

CHAPTER 14

SAM

I didn't have time to wash off my makeup and change out of my wig and dress (a copy of one of Bob Mackie's that I made myself). This wouldn't slow me down, though. I can move faster in an evening gown and heels than I can in a business suit and loafers.

One look at Tuwanda and I knew the situation was bad. Tuwanda doesn't show much emotion as a rule, but tonight the lines between her eyes and the grim set of her mouth told a different story.

I scanned the area, saw a couple of guys from Luke Air Force Base I knew, and waved at them. They seemed confused at first, but after they got a good look, they waved back.

"Who won tonight?" one of them called out.

He was referring to our weekly talent show at Kind of a Drag, a local club.

"Me, of course."

It's true. I only lost once, and that was because I went out on a limb and tried something different. I thought I made a great Hillary Clinton, but I was disqualified because two of the judges insisted I wasn't in drag.

But no one could beat my Cher impression. I was a great Liza Minnelli, too. A lot of the younger guys got their Lady Gaga on, but I preferred more of a challenge. Anyone can staple cold cuts together.

I'd called MJ and Beth, and they'd gotten the telephone tree started. They'd recruited a good-sized crowd. The experience and training of the group was inconsistent—we're not talking Navy SEALs or Army Rangers here—but what they lacked in expertise and experience, they more than made up for in determination. Kate was not someone who, in any of our minds, was expendable. Hell, not even a hair on her head was expendable, although some pieces of her wardrobe should be donated to third-world nations for use as tent material or fuel.

Tuwanda was doing her best to hang on, but I could see she was scared. She was quieter than usual and kept looking around as if she were afraid of something sneaking up on her.

I gave her a hug when I reached her, and she hugged me back long and hard.

When she released me, I asked her for a briefing. She didn't have much to add to what she had told me on the phone.

I don't believe in that spaceman and alien crap. My thinking is that if we got visitors from outer space, they'd watch *The Real Housewives of New York* and go screaming back to wherever they came from. Then, on their home planet, stories about the visit would evolve into myths about a breed of fighting trolls with red claws and enormous heads.

After a debate about who would go where and with whom, we divided into four groups, each of which was assigned to a sector of the neighborhood not yet covered by Tuwanda or Roderick. We promised to let each other know about any interesting developments.

MJ, Ralph, and I were in one group. Tuwanda and the Care Bares made up another group; Venus, Beth, and Larry made up group three; and Jane, Kate's mother, Eleanor, and the Stepford real-estate agents made up the fourth. Eleanor kept looking from me to MJ and then to Larry and back again, shaking her head. I was glad when we headed out in separate directions. The woman could make grass feel bad about being green.

CHAPTER 15

KATE

The room whirled and tipped, and my head throbbed. I recognized the familiar symptoms of a concussion.

I was assessing the severity of the concussion by comparing it to previous concussions, when I saw the alien.

My first impression was of a gelatinous monster with eight arms. One of them could have been a head. It was hard to tell.

The monster's innards were visible through transparent skin that reminded me of aspic.

He or she took a step—or a slither—toward me and crashed to the floor.

"Dammit," said the alien in what would be considered a male voice on Earth.

I was comforted by the alien's use of English. Since it had taken the time to learn our language—or at least swear words in our language—I figured he or she must care about establishing a relationship with us beyond probing.

I sat up with some effort.

"Do you need some help?" I asked.

The alien groaned in response, which I took as a yes.

I tried to butt-walk to the end of the bed, but the pain of movement was excruciating.

I noticed I was sitting on a double bed covered by a beige quilt. The room was small, was painted beige, and had a beige carpet and a single beige-draped window. A circa-1975 television was bolted to the wall in front of the bed.

Two tentacles grabbed the end of the bed. After repeated attempts to stand up, the alien had to leave it at sprawling its upper body over the foot of the bed—not exactly a position of strength.

"Thanks for the help," it said.

Great. A sarcastic alien.

"I asked if you needed help out of politeness. I'm in no condition to help you. I've got a concussion."

"You don't seem as if you have a concussion, but it's understandable why you think you might have one."

I was about to take issue with his diagnosis, when it occurred to me that the alien sounded suspiciously familiar.

"Have we met before?" I asked.

"Yeah. You were sitting in a tree with my dad the first time I saw you. I saw you again in court."

"Nelsen Jr.?" I asked. I took a more careful look at what I had assumed was an alien—an odd assumption during normal circumstances but a perfectly understandable one in light of the last twenty-four hours.

I noticed that the gelatinous skin had rubbed off in places and had left big, greasy stains on the bedspread.

Its internal organs looked odd too. They were more like a free-form interpretation of the subject by a third grader. The heart, in particular, was creative. It was a square green box with a smiley face.

Seeing where I was looking, the alien, or Nelsen, said, "My seven-year-old daughter made some modifications before I discovered what she was up to and confiscated her brushes and paint."

The alien then cleared its throat, which, to me, didn't seem to require clearing.

"Yes, it's I. But technically, I'm Nelsen now. You drop the *Jr.* once the senior passes on."

"Nice," I growled inhospitably. "You're covered with Vaseline, and what looks to be an intestine is strung over your shoulder. Yet you feel qualified to give me a grammar lesson."

"I can explain," he said.

A pleading tone had bled into his voice.

"I was at the bakery, er, looking for something. I heard you and the black lady come in."

"Tuwanda," I provided.

"And I hid in a storage room on the third floor. I cracked the door so I could watch what you were doing. Then the laser show started and scared the hell out of me. The part that really freaked me out, though, was just after, when I heard the footsteps."

Footsteps scared him more than death rays?

"You and Ruwanda ran to the other side of the building."

"Tuwanda," I corrected. "She's a person, not a country."

Nelsen continued without acknowledging my correction. "I followed you because I thought maybe you knew a way out that I didn't. I saw you boost Tamara—"

"Oh, for God's sake, it's Tuwanda," I interrupted.

"Up to the roof. You got up on the sill, and another one of those flashes went off."

"Did you see where it came from?"

"From the south. The beam showed for a nanosecond. It missed the building and went over a clump of paloverde trees. I don't know where it went after that.

"When the flash went off, you lost your balance, recovered it, saw me, and lost it again. You fell out the window. I thought for sure you were dead.

"The footsteps on the stairs stopped after the flash. When they started up again, they sounded like they were going downstairs fast.

"I heard a car start and drive away. It had to have been a truck, because I can recognize the sound of just about any car."

I raised an eyebrow questioningly.

"I worked at a toll booth for a summer. There wasn't much to do, so I memorized car sounds. Anyway, I waited a few minutes and then ran outside to check on you."

"You *waited* a few minutes? Nice," I said.

"Well, if I'd gotten zapped or kidnapped, I wouldn't be able to help either one of us," he shot back. "Anyway, I found you unconscious but still alive. Fortunately, you fell into a pile of mulch, and it softened your landing."

Strangely enough, this had happened to me before.

I sniffed my shirtsleeve and detected the unmistakable odor of mulch. It was likely for the garden behind the church and had been placed next to the bakery to spare church members from the smell.

"I dragged you to my car and brought you to my hotel room so you could recover. At some point during the dragging, you woke up, took a picture of me, said you were a white napkin and I shouldn't get you dirty, and then passed out again."

A napkin? Maybe my scrambled brain had been thinking about the mustard incident in Weiner's court.

"Why did you bring me here instead of the hospital?"

"Because then I would have to explain this," he said, sweeping his hand over his Vaseline-covered body.

When he lifted his arm, three more arms followed. I noticed they were connected to each other by thin plastic threads.

"How did you drag me with grease-covered tentacles?" I asked.

"I hooked my arms—my real arms—under your shoulders and pulled."

I inspected my shirt. The location of the grease marks supported his story.

"Go wash everything off, and then take me to the hospital."

"It's not as easy as you'd think. Based on experience, I have to wash and rinse at least five more times to get the Vaseline off. The organs are drawn with permanent Magic

Marker, but I could cover them with a shirt if I had one. Are you going to tell the police about this?"

"I have to, Nelsen, not only because kidnapping is a crime but also because I represent Deacon Davis. I don't know what you were looking for in the bakery, but it could be relevant to your dad's murder case."

"But—" Nelsen was interrupted by the sound of a key turning in the door lock.

"Do you know who that is?" I whispered.

Nelsen shook his head and stared apprehensively at the door.

We watched as the doorknob turned.

CHAPTER 16

The door swung open, and Mike Raymond walked in. He stopped short when he caught sight of us.

"What's going on here?" He sounded like a parent who'd walked in on his teenage daughter sitting on the couch way too close to a teenage boy.

Nelsen and I began to talk at once. Mike held up his hand.

"You go first," he said, pointing to Nelsen.

I imagined Nelsen sticking his tongue out at me. I couldn't tell if he actually did, because a Vaseline-covered tentacle mask covered his face. At least I think it was his face.

"I was searching the bakery—"

"Wait," commanded Raymond. "Is that you, Nelsen Jr.?"

"Yes," Nelsen affirmed. "But you have to drop the Jr. because my dad is dead."

Raymond switched his intense gaze to me.

"Have you been talking to my client without my consent?"

"After he kidnapped me without *my* consent, I spoke with him for the sole purpose of clarifying the situation," I snapped back.

Raymond looked confused. I didn't blame him.

"All right, let's all calm down and get this figured out," he said.

"You're the only one who needs to calm down," I retorted. "Nelsen and I were doing just fine until you burst in."

"Opening the door to my room with a key qualifies as bursting in?"

"I was talking to a man dressed like a Martian. I didn't know what to expect."

"You raise an interesting issue," he said, returning his gaze to Nelsen. "Why are you coated in Vaseline, and why do you have eight arms? Or maybe one's your head. It's hard to tell."

Nelsen told him a shorter version of what he'd told me. He didn't tell Raymond what he was looking for in the bakery either. But maybe Raymond already knew.

"Did you see anyone besides Kate and her friend at the bakery?" he asked.

"No. I did see a dark truck pass by going real slow. It took off after I dragged Kate to my car. I didn't see anyone get in or out of it. I figured it was just a curious local."

"Did you notice what kind of truck it was?" I asked.

"No. I worked the passenger lane at the tollbooth. Now, if it was a Kia—"

"Do not continue," I interrupted. I wasn't interested in Kias.

Realizing I wasn't going to get more out of Nelsen now that Mike was there, I reiterated a prior request.

"One of you needs to take me to a hospital."

"You look fine to me," said Mike.

"That's not the point. I fell out of a third-story window, for God's sake."

Mike looked at Nelsen for confirmation.

Nelsen nodded. "But a pile of mulch broke her fall."

"That explains a lot," said Mike, wrinkling his nose.

"If you don't get me out of here, I'll charge both of you with false imprisonment in addition to the charge against Nelsen for kidnapping."

"Are you up for a compromise?" asked Mike.

He went on without waiting for an answer.

"How about we drop you off at your house, and you don't file any charges against us?"

"That's not a compromise. It's a win for your side. Plus, I don't like the 'dropping off' part. It sounds like a threat."

"Okay then. Just let me and my client go outside and discuss our options."

"Take me home." I was tired, I hurt, and I didn't want to wait while these two bozos brainstormed—more like brain-drizzled.

CHAPTER 17

Mike left Nelsen in the room to shower and drove me to my condo in a low, hard-to-get-into car that sounded like a Harley. I did like the black horse on the steering wheel, though.

He dropped me off at the front curb of my condo building, just as he'd said he would, and no more.

I was too tired to object to the poor service and lousy manners. I figured the struggle to get out of the car would be twice the struggle to get in, which had involved me kneeling with my butt facing the car seat, falling into the car seat, and then swinging my legs in.

I rolled carefully onto the sidewalk.

"Do you need any help?" he asked, too late.

About all I can get, you nit.

I stifled this retort before it came out of my mouth, a heretofore-undiscovered capability. Instead, I stood up, shaking but holding my head high, and said, "No. I'm fine."

He left, stomping on the accelerator.

And to think that the first time I saw him, I felt some chemistry, I thought. *Maybe my mulch smell turned him off.*

Whatever had caused the chemistry to disappear was a force for good, because the guy was a jerk.

I charged into a few walls and tripped over a planter but eventually made it to my condo without additional serious injuries. I called Sam's mobile rather than falling into bed, which my body felt would have been a far better plan.

"Hi, Sam," I said when he picked up after a half ring.

There was silence at the other end except for what sounded like a crowd murmuring in the background. Maybe Sam was still at the costume party at Kind of a Drag.

I heard Sam scream, "It's Kate! She's alive!"

I was confused that the matter was in controversy.

Sam got back on the phone. "Where are you? We've been looking for you all night."

I glanced at the clock. It was three in the morning.

"I'm at my condo, but I just got here. Before that, I was kidnapped by an alien and held in a hotel room. I had a conversation with him and then with his lawyer."

"The alien had a lawyer? Sheesh. What is the galaxy coming to?"

"No, the alien turned out to be Nelsen Nelsen Jr., who is now plain Nelsen Nelsen because his dad died. Mike Raymond showed up later."

There was a pause on the other end.

"You hit your head again, didn't you?"

"Yes." My lower lip trembled, and I wanted to cry. "I fell out of a third-story window, but I landed in a pile of mulch, so I'm okay except for maybe a slight concussion, and I stink."

There was another pause. Sam was likely remembering a previous escapade when I had jumped off a fire escape into a pile of mulch.

"Sam?"

"I was thinking. What are the odds of falling out of a window into a pile of mulch twice?"

For the rest of the population, one in a billion. In my world, fifty-fifty.

I heard barking among the voices in the background.

"Is that Ralph?" The tears came and streamed down my face.

"Yup. He's the best searcher we have. He followed your trail to a set of tire tracks, so we figured the alien had a car. Then we went door to door looking for you in case the alien was a local. You have no idea how many times I've been threatened with a baseball bat in the last six hours."

"Who all is there?" I asked between snuffles.

Sam went through a list of the usual suspects—Tuwanda, MJ, Beth, etc.—but there were a few surprises.

"Jane and your mother were here for a while, and Bryan and Mark showed up about midnight. We had to separate them because Bryan kept calling Mark a cougar chaser, a gigolo, and the Biebs. Mark was cool about it at first, but after a while, he started to give Bryan tips on how to get in shape."

There's nothing that will cheer you up more than two men competing for you.

Sam put me on speakerphone, and I assured everyone that I was okay. Then I thanked them for all they had done, stopping now and then to blow my nose on my sleeve.

Sam took over as head spokesman again. "I know everyone wants to talk with Kate—"

"An' hug her," shouted out a voice I recognized as Tuwanda's.

"Yes, and hug her," Sam continued. "But she's going to need lots of rest. So give her a couple days to recover before you come to visit."

"Bullshit!" yelled Tuwanda.

"All right, new plan," said Sam. "Line up in front of me, and we'll work out a visiting schedule."

He went off speakerphone. "Kate, you don't need to stay on the line. If you feel up to it, though, could you call your mother and let her know you're alive and well?"

"Can't Tuwanda, MJ, or Beth do it?"

"Your mother got to MJ this morning. MJ feels like a failure because she's not married with kids at her age. The long and the short of it is that none of us will talk to your mother."

Damn.

"Okay, fine. I'll call her, even though every molecule in my body is screaming, 'Nononononono.'"

After Sam and I signed off, I looked up the hotel where my mother was staying and made the call, praying that she wasn't in or was so deeply asleep that she wouldn't hear the phone ring.

A chipper-sounding operator answered. "Could you put me through to Eleanor Williams in room four twenty-two?" I asked, hoping he would say, "No. absolutely not," even though the odds were against me.

He put me straight through.

My mother answered after four rings. Plan A had failed. I had no plan B.

"Hello?" she asked, sounding groggy.

"Hi, Mom. It's Kate."

"Kate? It's about time. I've been so worried about you. You don't know what you put me through. It was so hot. I was already perspiring when we arrived at that godforsaken neighborhood, and then Sam told us he wanted us to walk through that filthy slum and look for you. I was so grateful when that nice Jane suggested we sit in her car with the AC on for a bit. She had a thermos of cold lemonade and poured it into lovely little teacups. I thought the teacups were such a nice touch.

"We got caught up in a conversation about how poor people made their own beds and should lie in them and how good, hard work was the key to success. Dear, Jane and I have so much in common."

Good, hard work? My mother had worked at a travel agency for less than a week. I don't mean to imply that child raising is an easy job, but Mom hadn't done much of that either.

"The time just flew by—did you know that Jane knows the governor?—and then we noticed that everyone was gone. Since we had no idea how to find them, Jane was nice enough to take me back to my hotel. I was so exhausted that I fell asleep without taking my eye makeup off."

She said this last part in a tone implying it would be my fault if she woke up later with smeared mascara.

Mom paused and then said, "But that is a mother's burden."

What—smeared mascara? Lemonade?

"I'd love to keep chatting, but I need my rest. I'll touch base tomorrow. Maybe we can meet for lunch."

Click.

Not once did she ask what had happened or how I was doing. I didn't take offense, though. I was used to this, and any conversation with Mom that ended quickly was a good one.

I headed for my bedroom, passed on a shower, and crawled underneath the covers. Everything whirled when I closed my eyes.

Make up your mind, I snarled at my brain. *Either whirl when I open my eyes, or whirl when I close my eyes. You can't have it both ways.*

I opened my eyes, hoping the whirling would stop under the either/or theory.

My vision was clear—so clear that I could see every detail of the weird thing standing, floating, slithering, or whatever it was doing at the foot of my bed.

"Dammit, Nelsen. Stop it. That's not funny. Let me sleep."

Nelsen did not respond, so I got out of bed and tottered toward him as threateningly as I could, but the tottering part canceled out most of the threatening part. As I got closer, I noticed that Nelsen had gotten a new costume. This one must have been made by a professional costumer. It was incredibly realistic—not that I know what constitutes realistic when it comes to aliens.

I was closing in on Nelsen, when one of his tentacles shot out, and I felt a slight sting on my arm.

CHAPTER 18

TUWANDA

As soon as I left South Phoenix, I headed for Kate's condo. Damn that Sam, makin' us sign up on a schedule an' all. I woulda been first, too, if MJ hadn't hip-bumped me halfway to California. It don't make a difference, though. Bein' a free spirit an' all, I'm not much for schedules.

I didn't want to bother Kate. I jus' wanted to check with my own eyes as to how she was doin'. Sometimes Kate underplays how she feelin' so she don't bother people with her problems. I don't know how she got that way, but she sure as hell didn't get it from her mom. That woman gets a paper cut an' says, "Oh, it's nothing. I got it because I was trying to find the card from Kate's cousin so Kate could read it. Her cousin is a well-known surgeon, you know. But don't bother with li'l ole me. I'll be okay. By the way, do you have something I could use to stop the bleeding? And perhaps some Bactine for the infection? I think I may have to lie down on the couch."

I parked my car and rode the elevator up to Kate's floor. Her front door was locked. I din't want to knock an' disturb her, so I picked the lock like I always do.

It was real quiet inside. I figured she must be sleepin', so I tiptoed back to her bedroom so's not to wake her up. I peeked in an' saw somethin' leave through the window—fast. I just got a glimpse of it, but it looked like a damned alien.

I was sick of aliens.

I looked at the bed, but Kate wasn't in it. I walked aroun' the bed, and I found her lyin' on the floor.

I din't have time to be shocked or scared. I had to put that off till later.

I called 911, told 'em where to come, and suggested they haul ass.

I knelt next to Kate and felt for a pulse. I wasn't findin' any. I started shakin' an' cryin' an' alternatin' between prayin' an' givin' God what for.

I heard someone come in an' thought maybe the EMTs had rocket packs to get here so fast.

It was Sam.

"What's going on?" he demanded. "Your visiting time isn't until tomorrow afternoon."

I couldn't say nothin' back to him 'cause of the cryin', so I just pointed to Kate.

Sam bolted over an' did the same thing I done, except his face turned white, which is somethin' white folks have the advantage on. Ain't no amount of shock could turn me white. You gotta look for other cues.

Sam grabbed a blanket off the bed and tucked it in around Kate. "Did you call 911?"

"First thing."

"How long ago?"

"Maybe five minutes."

I heard a gasp behind me and turned around to find MJ. She musta crept up while Sam and I were talkin'.

Sam looked at her sternly. "Your time slot is not until tomorrow morning."

"Fuck off, you type-A, control-freak twit. Why is Kate lying there looking so, so—"

One look at our faces and MJ knew it was bad.

Beth showed up next, usin' as her excuse that she rode over with MJ.

Then the EMTs walked in. One of 'em felt Kate's pulse an' then looked at the other two, shakin' his head. He and another EMT started pullin' equipment out of a bag, and the third one left. One of guys workin' the equipment had a badge sayin' Keith Wilson, Supervisor. Keith tol' us to go stand in the other room because they needed space to work.

We walked with our heads down into the living room. In my mind, I was sayin', *Dear God, no.* I din't like that EMT shakin' his head at all. That's the shit they do on TV when someone din't make it.

"Sam, do you think she's de—" MJ started to ask.

Everyone screamed, "No," cuttin' her off before she said that nasty word. We was all thinkin' it, but thinkin' ain't the same as sayin'. Unless you're a politician, sayin' stuff out loud makes it more real.

Mark and Bryan showed up, elbowing each other for front position. Mark had the physical advantage, but Bryan, cuz he's older an' wiser, outstrategized Mark and pulled into the lead.

They stopped cold when they saw us.

"You look like you're sitting shivah," said Mark jokingly. His ice-blue eyes didn't look like they got the joke, though.

He got serious real fast. "Where's Kate?"

"She's in her bedroom with the EMTs. They tol' us to wait out here."

I din't have time to go into too much detail, cuz the third EMT burst through the front door, pushin' a gurney.

We all shouted out questions about Kate, but he jus' shook his head an' kept on pushin' till he got next to Kate.

Man, I hated that head-shakin' stuff.

A couple minutes later, they rolled her out. She was attached by tubes and wires to all sorts of plastic bags and electronic stuff. One of the EMTs scooted the monitors and IV stand alongside the gurney.

We tried to follow 'em out the door, but Mr. Wilson said, "No ride-alongs in the ambulance."

The EMT pushin' at the back end of the gurney said, "John C. Lincoln Hospital," just before he disappeared into the hallway.

After we heard the elevator doors open and close, everyone turned to look at me.

I tol' them about findin' Kate and callin' 911. I didn't mention seein' the alien.

"Was anyone else in the room when you got there?" asked Bryan in his cop-interviewin'-a-witness voice.

Damn him. "Yes," I said, not lookin' anyone in the eyes. "I saw either a man dressed like an alien or an alien jump out the window."

"Which window?" demanded MJ.

"The one in Kate's room."

Everyone got quiet. We all knew Kate's apartment pretty good, and there ain't no balcony off the bedroom window— just air.

Like one big amoeba, we moved into Kate's room and looked out the window. We din't see no body or stain on the concrete below.

Bryan asked, "Tuwanda, how much sleep have you gotten in the last two days?"

CHAPTER 19

KATE

I didn't know what place this was, but light was everywhere—not glaring searchlights or those horrible fluorescent lights that age you twenty years, but softly glowing light. I didn't know where I was, but I felt wonderful. I hadn't felt that good since—actually, I'd never felt that good.

People's shadows were moving about. I say "shadows" because there were no people attached to them. The scene reminded me of Peter Pan losing his shadow and Wendy having to sew it back on once they found it. Maybe the shadows' people were searching for them.

I looked down at myself, and I was a shadow too.

I couldn't remember anything. I had no past and no clue about, or fear of, the future. I didn't care. I just wanted to keep feeling the way I did.

A whirling mass of darkness was situated in the middle of the space the shadows occupied. Every so often, I felt something pull me toward it. I resisted because I noticed that the other shadows were carefully avoiding it.

I found it strange that I could use my shadow strength to stay away. *Peter Pan* notwithstanding, you'd think a shadow wouldn't have the ability to do much of anything except go wherever the breeze—or vortex—took it.

A nonshadow appeared and moved toward me. It was strange looking yet somehow familiar. Its tentacles moved slowly, as if it were walking underwater.

I wasn't afraid of the nonshadow. As I said, fear was no longer part of my emotional repertoire.

When the creature got close, it gently wrapped its tentacles around me and held me like a mother holds a baby. It led me to the vortex and pushed me in.

CHAPTER 20

MARK

We left for the hospital, taking two cars because Bryan wouldn't sit in the same car with me.

I sure wish Bryan would stop calling me Marky Mark. Who the hell is Marky Mark anyway?

The guy just won't let go of the fact that Kate likes me. He thinks like an old man. Times have changed. People date more than one person these days, and Kate's hot. She should have four or five datable guys in her contact list.

I wasn't sure what was going on, but everyone looked scared and upset, and nobody said a word on the way to the hospital. The EMTs rolled Kate out of her condo so fast that I didn't have a chance to see much. It probably didn't matter. She had tubes coming out of her mouth and an oxygen mask, so even if I'd gotten a better look at her, I still wouldn't have seen much.

Kate is not going to die. She's the toughest woman I know. She's had more concussions than a defensive lineman, and each time she gets knocked on the head, she shakes it off and keeps going. I was in a special-ops unit in Iraq, and if one of the guys in my unit got into the ring with her, I'd put my money on Kate.

If she's going to be okay, why am I shaking? God, I feel sick.

CHAPTER 21

BRYAN

What's Mark, that freak of nature, hanging around for? If he thinks for one minute that he's going to be the first face Kate sees when she wakes up, he's in error.

I don't care if the guy has abs like Ryan Gosling, arms like a Russian weightlifter, and a bubble butt you could bounce a brick off of—Mr. Universe isn't Kate's type.

Kate and I have a common history. We're soul mates.

I admit I haven't been around lately with the election taking up so much of my time. Still, I thought our connection was strong enough to weather the stress of a political campaign.

I rode with Sam and MJ to the hospital. We cut ten minutes off our travel time with MJ at the wheel. As an officer of the law, I should have made her go the speed limit, but I was too worried about Kate, and the sooner we got to the hospital, the better.

I hoped Beth was driving the car Mark was in. If she was, a drive that should have taken twenty minutes would take an hour.

I wish Kate understood how much I love her, and believe me, she's not an easy person to love. I don't know what happened to her during her childhood, her adolescence, or her adulthood before she moved to Phoenix. She won't talk about any of it, but whatever it was destroyed her ability to trust. As soon as you get close to her, she stops making eye contact and distances herself with jokes—or distance. But she's got a heart of gold and will do anything to help a friend or stranger. Plus, she sees value in everyone. Kate doesn't believe in caste systems based on income level, sex, religion, intelligence, culture, race, education, job, or background, and the conglomerate of friends she's assembled is more than evidence of her egalitarian approach to humanity.

Kate would do anything for us, and we would do anything for Kate too.

The withdrawing and the caring aspects of her personality represent opposite ends of the emotional spectrum, though. I considered the possibility that she was bipolar, but usually her reactions vary predictably with the circumstances.

We asked for Kate's status as soon as we got to the emergency room.

The nurse on duty shook her head. "There's no change of status on Ms. Williams."

"Could you tell us what the status is that hasn't changed?" I asked.

"Yes. Ms. Williams was dead when she arrived, and she is still dead."

CHAPTER 22

MJ

That nurse was either lying or got Kate confused with someone else. Kate is a force of nature. Forces of nature don't die.

My legs gave out, and I joined Bryan and Sam, who were already sitting on the floor.

Mark, Beth, and Tuwanda burst through the double glass doors into the ER. Tuwanda stopped when she saw us. She opened her mouth, but no words came out.

I looked at her through the tears streaming from my eyes and said, "She's dead."

Their shock was written on their faces. As in our case, the strength went out of their legs. Mark and Tuwanda sat, and Beth fainted.

This couldn't be happening.

Sam and I have always been different—the kind of different that most law firms and government departments and agencies don't like to hire. I talk tough, but the mean things people say about my hair, tattoos, fashion sense, and weight hurt. Sure, Sam jokes a lot about my clothes, but he takes it as well as he gives it, so it doesn't bother me.

I couldn't think of any employer who would hire a paralegal that looks like me and let her investigator wear six-inch Jimmy Choo heels in the office.

Without Kate, Sam, me, and Beth, the Bible thumper, would be at each other's throats. Kate was the glue that held us together. Each of us is 100 percent loyal to her and would do anything for her.

We weren't there in time to save her this time. I don't think I'll ever forgive myself for that.

CHAPTER 23

TUWANDA

This ain't happenin'. God, I most always defer to your decision-makin' ability, but this time, I gotta take issue with you.

What the hell? You let all them dingbats in Congress live, but you take away our Kate? That's a bad decision.

Jus' sit down with a glass of wine, relax, rethink what you did, an' change your mind.

Kate's my best friend, God. I never had a best friend before Kate come along.

I've been judged all my life, and she don't judge.

CHAPTER 24

KATE

My head was killing me, and someone was talking loudly, which made it hurt worse. I wanted to open my eyes but was too tired. Why couldn't I go back to the shadow room? I didn't like this noisy, hurtful place.

I focused on the voice, hoping it would give me a clue as to where I was. The voice was slow and solemn and mentioned Christ's name quite a bit. I didn't recognize it.

Another voice interrupted the slow, solemn one.

"Why he doin' last rites? She dead. It's too late." A big, wet sob followed. "Besides"—*sob*—"Kate's Presbyterian. I don't think this sh—stuff works on Presbyterians. She got—"

I recognized this voice—it was Tuwanda's.

A man's voice overrode Tuwanda's, and I flinched at the increased volume. I identified the voice as that belonging to Mark.

"I called Kate's mom at her hotel. She said she had to take a shower and do her hair and makeup but would come over when she was done."

"She flinched," whispered Beth. At least I assumed it was Beth since she's the only one I know who whispers.

"What? What are you saying?" boomed Mark excitedly.

I flinched again.

The room erupted in shouts for a nurse or doctor.

I heard running steps. Then a woman said, "Please quiet down. You're disturbing the other patients. I've notified the doctor, and he'll be here soon to explain."

"Explain what?" demanded MJ.

"If I told you, I would be practicing medicine without a license."

"You're a nurse. What are you doing here if you're not practicing medicine?" Bryan said.

"Hello," said a new voice. "I'm Dr. Schlauterhaus."

"No way," muttered MJ.

"Nurse Farter told me one of you saw the decedent move."

Farter? Seriously?

Somebody snickered—probably Sam.

"I saw her twitch the first time," said Beth.

"We all saw it the second time," said Bryan.

He placed his fingers over my wrist for a nanosecond. "No pulse," he announced.

There was a pause during which I pictured the doctor stroking his chin and looking serious.

"Sometimes electrical impulses from nerves will cause the body to jerk or twitch postmortem. I've seen it many times."

"Why's that? Cuz all your patients die?" mumbled Tuwanda. Speaking much louder, she added, "I want you to hook up one of them machines to see if Katie has a heartbeat."

There must have been something in her look, because the doctor agreed. I heard a click and felt a blood pressure cuff being wrapped around my upper arm.

The cuff inflated immediately.

"What's that?" said MJ excitedly.

"I-it must be a machine malfunction," said Dr. Schlauterhaus. "Nurse, could you bring in the heart monitor from station two?"

Less than a minute later, I heard Nurse Farter roll in the heart monitor from station two.

I got a different cuff, but otherwise, the experience was the same.

"Ha!" the onlookers chorused.

"Even so, with her brain being deprived of oxygen for so long, she will be largely nonfunctional," said the doctor, not wanting to be proven entirely wrong.

The nearly constant talking was not helping my headache. I covered my ears, which did little to keep the sound out.

"Look at that," said Mark. "She's alive. My love is alive!"

Bryan's reaction was immediate. "Shut the fuck up, boy toy! She's not your love. She's *my* love."

"I don't think arguing is appropriate under the circumstances," said Beth in her firm, schoolteacher voice.

"Kate," Beth said in a kinder voice, "can you talk?"

Tuwanda took my hand between hers and gave it a squeeze.

"I have a killer headache," I mumbled, slitting one eye open.

Beth began crying and praising Jesus.

Tuwanda whispered, "I knew it. Katie can't die. Not on our watch."

"Where were you?" asked MJ.

Beth stopped praising to listen to my answer, and everyone leaned in.

"With the shadow people and the alien," I answered.

The doctor snorted in an I-told-you-so kind of way.

CHAPTER 25

After a short but intense discussion between doctor and nurse, they decided to push the code-blue button because there is no code for resurrection. They herded everyone out of my room just in time for a crowd of doctors, nurses, and techs to take their places.

IVs were reinserted, and more of my blood was taken. X-rays and an MRI were redone. Every inch of my body was prodded and examined, during which I was peppered with questions to test my mental acuity.

I was missing the shadow place during this commotion. The sense of joy and peace I'd experienced there was a far cry from the human pincushion I'd become.

Hey, wait a minute, I thought. *Could that be the same thing Nelsen Sr. experienced when the aliens took him? No wonder he was so hot to go back.*

The army of hospital personnel finally left, although paranoia being part of my makeup, I figured they were congregating outside the door to plan the next battery of tests.

Just as I had feared, the door opened.

I yelled, "Get out, you barbarians! You stick another needle in me and I will put a hit out on you. I know people who would do it."

It was unfortunate that I still had a tube in my throat, as everything that came out was unintelligible.

The hospital staff had turned off the lights in my room, so when the door closed behind my visitor, I couldn't make out a thing.

The aroma of Chanel No. 5 filled my nostrils.

"Tuwanda! Thank God it's you," I said, which came out as "Tiwawa! Fank gof iss oo."

"Girl, I'm glad to see you too." She turned on the lamp next to my bed.

I looked at her questioningly. At least I think it did. It was hard to know with the throat and nose tubes covering my face.

"In my bidness, you have to talk all the time with somethin' in your mouth, so you understan' the language."

I nodded sympathetically.

"So you wanna tell me about the shadow people and the alien?"

I told Tuwanda as best I could. She didn't interrupt by asking me to repeat anything, despite my garbled presentation. She seemed to understand everything.

When I finished, she said, "I 'member you tellin' me Nelsen Sr. really liked bein' with the aliens. Maybe that's where you were too—on a spaceship. I don't think you went to heaven. It don't sound like heaven at all. Heaven's got angels, lots of food, an' a big-ass swimmin' pool."

Mention of Nelsen and a swimming pool triggered an association. "Nelsen sat in his tree at night from ten to midnight. Maybe he didn't call 911 when he saw Tiffany floating face down. Maybe he watched her drown."

Tuwanda nodded. "If he saw her drown and didn't do a damn thing to save her, maybe the guilt's been buildin' up all these years until he can't take it no more, so he hangs hisself?"

"It could have happened that way. It also could be that he saw someone drown her, and whoever it is didn't want him saying anything."

"Why din't he say somethin' to the police earlier? Or why wasn't he killed earlier?"

That was a stumper.

"You're right. It's pure conjecture at this point."

"You say that like all the other shit we been talkin' about is hard facts."

"True. Somehow I feel responsible, though."

"Are you sayin' Nelsen Sr.'s death was all *your* fault? Damn, your mama messed you up big-time. Are you still apologizin' to furniture an' shit?"

I had a habit of saying, "Sorry," every time I bumped into an inanimate object.

"No. Not furniture," I lied. "I still apologize to glassware but only when I break it."

Tuwanda rolled her eyes. "Please get help."

I made a limited gesture to the tubes and wires—limited because the end points of most of the tubes and wires were my wrists. "I'm getting about as much help as I can handle," I snarled, which only made the garbling worse.

"You got that right."

Right on cue, we heard voices in the hallway.

"I better get outta here," whispered Tuwanda. "Rest as much as you can, Katie."

"I will," I whispered, which actually cut down on the garbling. "I want you to get me out of here tomorrow."

"I feel another Kate adventure comin'." Tuwanda made it sound as if that were the worst possible thing that could happen, but the sparkle in her eyes belied her tone.

CHAPTER 26

I slept reasonably well that night despite the nursing staff waking me up every hour to check my vitals and to check my wires and tubes because I periodically unclipped my blood pressure, heart, and pulse monitors.

My breathing tube had been removed in the early evening, leaving me with a sore throat. I didn't mind the sore throat so much, though, because it distracted me from the pain in my head.

After the 6:00 a.m. nurse left, a phlebotomist came in for what I was sure would be the first of many blood tests, unless Tuwanda came through.

"Which arm do you want me to use?"

"Neither. Thank God you're here, Tuwanda. We need to move fast because someone will be in to serve breakfast at six thirty."

"Anythin' good? I could wait if they servin' somethin' good, like pancakes with lots of syrup."

"You've been in enough hospitals to know that it's never any good," I snapped.

"Okay, okay, take it easy. I liked you better when you had that tube shoved down your throat."

I started to pull off monitor wires.

"Watchoo doin'?" asked Tuwanda, turning up the volume but still in the whispering range. "You gonna bring everyone at the nurses' station running. They'll think you're dead again. We got to roll them machines along with us."

"No, we don't. I've been lowering their expectations all night. They'll just think I turned over and pulled everything out again. Besides, how did you plan to explain why a dead body was attached to monitors?"

"I'd tell 'em they was just in case you rose from the dead again."

I tried to sit up, but Tuwanda pushed me back down.

"For purposes of this phase of the plan, you need to lie still, cuz you dead. I'm gonna roll you out of this room and make like I'm heading for the morgue."

"What are the other phases?"

"I'm gonna take you to the morgue. They got an unloading bay for, um, corpses, an' I know the guy who operates the door to the bay. He's one of Black Diamond's regulars and owes me money. I tol' him he does this little favor for me, and we'll be square."

"Who is Black Diamond?"

"She's a new hire. She got tired of bein' beat by her pimp, so now she's workin' for Care Bares."

Tuwanda pulled the sheet over my head.

"Okay, here we go. Stay as still as you can."

Tuwanda is an expert at many things, but she is not good at pushing a gurney in a straight line. I felt like the steel ball in a pinball game. A person with less experience in being dead could not have pulled it off and would have jumped off the first time Tuwanda cut a corner and slammed his or her elbow into a doorframe.

God only knows how, but she got me in the service elevator with no one stopping her and asking her who she had on the cart and why she was abusing a corpse.

That was where our luck ended. One floor down, the elevator stopped, and someone else got on.

"Who's that you got there?" asked either a deep-voiced man or a really deep-voiced woman.

"Kate Williams, poor soul. Takin' her to the morgue."

"She died again?"

"Yes. But this time, she ain't comin' back. Doctors think her alive time was some kinda fluke, and they lookin' to dissect every little bit of her to find out what happened. Then they gonna publish an article on it and get famous."

"Ain't that just the way it always is?" commented the deep voice. "They don't give a shit about postpeople unless they can write a paper on 'em."

The elevator doors slid open again, and Mr. Deep Voice and Tuwanda told each other to have a good day.

"I don't see how you can have a good day with me being dead," I grumbled.

Tuwanda shushed me and slapped my arm.

"Lighten up the touch. Do you want to kill me again?" Playing dead was making me cranky.

The elevator stopped, and the doors slid open again. This time, Tuwanda turned the gurney around. She must have shoved it hard, because I bounced off the wall opposite the elevator and rebounded right back into the elevator.

"You accomplished nothing," I said, pointing out the obvious.

"Dammit, be quiet. I hear someone comin'."

I listened and heard faint footsteps approaching us.

I clammed up and listened as the footsteps grew louder and then stopped.

"Where are you going?" demanded a football linebacker of a nurse. I couldn't see her, but she sounded large. Plus, she was probably one of those busybodies who had to follow the rules and make sure everyone else did too.

I wondered if she was a relative.

"This must be the cadaver the FBI came to pick up," she announced stridently, implying "The world is in order because I made it so."

Tuwanda started to take issue with Linebacker's assumption but clammed up when she said, "They are waiting at the loading dock for you. You must be Tuwanda, correct? And this must be the twice-dead Caitlin Williams?"

I did the math and figured out I was still supposed to be dead.

"Why, yes," said Tuwanda as if butter could melt in her mouth. "She gonna be autopsied by the FBI to see what she's got that's so special. They lookin' for a resurrection gene.

I'm goin' with cuz she's my best friend in the whole world, and I want to supervise."

She was too far away to pinch, and I knew that reaching out to cover the distance might destroy the illusion of death, so I had to settle with being pleased with her characterization of me as her best friend and being disgusted by what she felt her duty as a best friend was.

The gurney started moving again. I could tell that the linebacker had taken over, because it did not veer off course and sailed around corners without damage to its passenger.

We passed through a door. The air was fresher and warmer on the other side.

"Agent Lackey and Agent Sheist, here are your passengers," announced Linebacker, as if by her meager involvement, she'd solved the world's problems, and thanks were due.

I heard Tuwanda's quick intake of breath. Something was wrong.

"Hello, um, gentlemen," she stuttered.

I guessed that she didn't recognize the two agents. I wasn't alarmed. They were likely friends of her friend, because Sheist had to be a made-up name.

"Do you need any help loading her?" asked Linebacker.

"As a matter of fact, we *could* use some help," said Lackey.

"Why, certainly. Stand back, gentlemen."

Before I knew it, the gurney was flattened, and I was lifted and then slid into the back of a vehicle.

I heard the door start to close, but then Tuwanda said, "Wait! I gotta ride with my bes' friend. Tha's what friends do."

Along with supervising said friend's autopsy. Ugh.

The vehicle started—by the noise it made, it was most certainly a truck—and we were on our way somewhere. I heard Tuwanda moving around for a bit, and then she lifted the sheet and peered down at me.

"I don't know these guys. All I know is they ain't friends of Pony."

"I take it Pony is the friend who was going to pick us up?"

"Yeah. We call 'im Pony 'cause he's a bookie an' he's always askin' people to pony up."

"How can you tell they're not friends of Pony?"

"Pony don't know people who look like that. They white, an' they wearin' suits that have federal agent written all over 'em."

I panicked. Tuwanda is phenomenal at sizing people up.

"I don't mean their suits liter'ly have *federal agent* written all over 'em. I mean they wearin' black business suits like the kind they sell at Men's Wearhouse. Ain't no self-respectin' black person goes to Macy's. You go to the Dollar Store or Niemen's, and there ain't nothin' in between."

"You're racist," I mumbled.

"Naw. Us blacks can say anythin' about each other, but if a white person say the same thing, they ain't gettin' home that night."

"So if Pony didn't send them, then what are they doing?"

"I was makin' up a story before about your bein' transported for tests, but I'm thinkin' it may be what's really happenin'."

"Maybe they got wind of the alien thing. I know! They're the Men in Black."

We both chuckled over that one. Then something occurred to me, and I stopped in midchuckle.

"Can they hear us back here?" I whispered.

"Not anymore. I found two teensy cameras and a couple overhearing thingys in here. While I was lookin' at 'em, the little wires got unhooked, and the batteries fell out. It's jus' sad how doohickey quality has gone downhill."

"So what do we do now? What happens when the truck stops and they come to get us?"

"We gotta think about that."

We both fell silent and thought.

After about a minute, Tuwanda said, "I got nothin'."

I didn't have much more than that.

"Maybe I can keep playing dead, and after they park me someplace, I'll find you, and we'll break out of wherever we are."

"Tha's pretty lame, but at least it's somethin'. We've got out of some pretty bad shit. This can't be worse than anythin' we already been through."

It was a good thing we had a plan, even a lame plan, because the truck slowed, turned sharply, and then stopped a few seconds later.

Tuwanda barely had enough time to cover my head with the sheet before the back doors swung open. I went back to playing dead, debating whether I should have rigor mortis or not. I chided myself for not watching more *CSI* episodes.

I was rolled into a cold room and parked. Then the door slammed shut. I raised an edge of the sheet and looked around. I was alone in a large concrete-block room. What little light there was came through a narrow, dirty window. The source was probably a yard or streetlight.

I pushed the sheet off my head and peered into the semidarkness. Stacked cardboard boxes lined the walls of the room, except for the wall in front of me, which was dominated by a huge, rolling metal garage door.

I was in a warehouse. Talk about lack of creativity. I've landed in the room of a senile elderly woman who insisted that I dress in ballet clothes. I can't tell you how many police, FBI, or sheriff interrogation rooms I've been in. Then there was the time I ended up in an emergency room with a pill-popping doctor. Waking up in a hotel room with Nelsen Jr. in his alien costume was high on the originality scale. But warehouses figured into most, if not all, television cop shows.

I sat up and, pivoting on my butt, swung my legs so that my feet hit the floor. The floor felt dirty and cold but was otherwise unremarkable. Dispensing with attempts to be quiet, I strolled to the door and tried the knob. The door swung open.

That made sense. Why lock in a dead person?

It took a few seconds for my eyes to adjust to the light, and I was able to get my bearings. I was standing at the end of a long corridor. Midway down was a line of five glass-fronted offices. Only three of the offices were lit, and in each of these, the curtains had been drawn shut.

I sidled up to the first office, having perfected the art of sidling during my tenure in Phoenix. I looked into the room through a crack between the curtains and saw an MIB talking to a man wearing shabby, stained clothes and a tinfoil fedora from the top of which jutted a wire coat hanger like a jaunty feather. The men were sitting on either side of a government-issue gray metal desk. I could not hear their voices, but whenever Metal Hat moved his lips, MIB wrote something on the legal pad in front of him.

And the government can't find ways to cut employment costs.

In the next office, a similar scene was playing out, except that the interviewee had shaped Reynolds Wrap into an intricate pirate hat with Christmas-tree tinsel glued around the edges like a sombrero—a hat of mixed lineage.

I couldn't see their faces, because both were intently focused on a piece of paper that looked, from where I stood, like an advertising flyer.

Sombrero Guy seemed familiar somehow. Suddenly, he looked up and straight at me. I ducked, but he'd already seen me.

"Mom!" he screamed joyously.

It was Larry, my son.

The door burst open, and the MIB rushed out.

"Kate?" he asked uncertainly.

I rose from my semicrouching position to face him.

"Yes. It is I," I answered, hoping to get points for good grammar. "Hello, Carter."

Carter was an agent of Homeland Security. I'd met him a few months ago, when he and two other agents—CIA and FBI—were interviewing me about a fantasy gang of guns for hire. Carter and I had experienced some brief chemistry at the time.

"Geez, Kate. I'm sorry I haven't called you. I've been so busy."

Does he think I was stalking him because he hasn't called?

"No problem. I've been busy myself," I said, looking pointedly down at my hospital gown.

Tuwanda had missed one little detail—she hadn't brought me my clothes.

The thought of Tuwanda reminded me of my original purpose.

"I'm looking for Tuwanda. Is she here?"

"Tuwanda?" he asked, looking confused.

Then I remembered that he had not met Tuwanda during our last escapade.

"A tall, gorgeous black woman in a Chanel jogging suit."

"Oh, *her*. She's hard to miss. Would you be insulted if I asked for her number?"

"Where is she?" I snapped.

Larry, who had been listening to this exchange in fascination, raised his hand. I do not raise impolite children.

"Yes, Larry?"

"She's in that office there," he said, pointing to the last office.

I pushed by Carter and headed toward it.

"Uh, Mom? You should probably close the back of your nightie," said Larry helpfully.

I grabbed the ends of the offensive piece of nonclothing and held them together with one hand. I banged on the fifth office's door with my free hand.

I slid under the arm of the man opening the door and found Tuwanda slumped in a chair, her chin resting against her chest.

"Tuwanda! Are you okay?" I screamed in alarm

She raised her head and gave me a loopy grin. Her eyes were all pupil.

I turned to the man who'd opened the door. "What did you give her?" I demanded.

"A mild barbiturate," he said.

"That's an oxymoron," I said, feeling for Tuwanda's pulse. "You shouldn't have given her anything. Her system has a hard time handling drugs."

Actually, her system loves drugs, which is why Tuwanda stays away from everything but aspirin.

Her pulse was slow, but at least it was there.

"What kind of barbiturate was it?" I asked, wanting to know what to tell the EMTs when I called.

The agent with Tuwanda hesitated and then said, "Scopolamine."

"Truth serum? Are you serious? The effect of that stuff has been scientifically disproven over and over again. The only thing it does is cause people to talk incessantly about stuff that may or may not be true."

"I'm old school, and I'm good at what I do," said the agent.

Tuwanda stirred. "Well, tha's half true. You is old," she said, and then she collapsed into giggles at her own joke.

"Who are you anyway?" demanded the agent.

"Who are *you*?" I snapped.

"I'm Agent Culpepper. Your turn."

"She's Kate Williams," provided Carter, who had followed me in and then hung around to watch the action.

Tuwanda, who was clearly on a roll, commented, "Culpepper? Shit. Are you some kinda plantation owner? Or maybe you own a fried-chicken fast-food chain? That reminds me—damn, I'm hungry."

Culpepper ignored her. I think maybe he was rethinking scopolamine's effectiveness.

"Fried chicken is awful good," continued Tuwanda, her stream-of-conscious monologue unabated by Culpepper's cold reception.

"'Specially that crispy kind they got down at Piece of Heaven."

Everyone in Phoenix knew about the fried chicken at Piece of Heaven. Five mouths started to water.

"Mom," said Larry, "I sure would like some of that chicken. Can you take me an' my friends to Piece of Heaven?"

I've learned from experience that any reference by Larry to "friends" likely meant the imaginary people in his head.

Culpepper rolled his eyes. "Why does he keep calling you Mom?"

"It's a real long story, but I'm gonna make it short for you, and I won't use no long words, cuz I know most feds barely made it through the first volume of the Dick and Jane series. You know the one where Spot's introduced? You miss that first book and the whole plot falls apart cuz you don't know who the hell Spot is."

"I'd prefer that Kate tell me the story," said Culpepper.

"Larry was a suspect in a murder case, and I was appointed his guardian ad litem for purposes of the court proceedings. I tried to explain to Larry what that meant, and in the following question-and-answer session, Larry compared a guardian to a mom, and I may have positively reinforced the comparison since it was the closest he'd come to understanding the guardian ad litem thing."

"I can see that happening," Carter said sincerely. As the result of his interview of Larry, he knew something about how Larry's mind worked.

That thought reminded me of something. "Why were you talking to Larry, Carter?"

Carter looked at Culpepper and said, "She was listening. She probably already knows about the laser."

I did know about the laser but only because Sam had told me.

"And another thing, Kate. Carter is my last name. My first name is Leslie."

Everyone stifled a giggle. Leslie pretended not to notice. "Most people call me Les."

Thank God.

He plowed forward, ignoring his audience's clear lack of priorities. "Because a weapons-grade laser was used in the attack on you at the old bakery, the NSA, CIA, FBI, and Pentagon are involved in an investigation to determine who gained access to the laser and how."

I raised my eyebrows. "And for this, you need to interrogate men wearing tinfoil hats?"

"The men in tinfoil hats know more about this town than anyone else. Of course you need to do some discounting for their interpretation of events, but other than that, the information is solid.

"I'll bet you didn't know that Larry and Jacob—the guy you saw in the first room—were in the area the night the, er, situation occurred."

I turned to Larry in surprise. "Why were *you* there?"

"I knew Nelsen. So did Jacob. We wanted to come down and lay flowers at the site of his demise. When we got there, we realized we forgot the flowers. Then a bright—and I mean *bright*—light flashed like lightning. We knew it wasn't gonna rain, because we checked the Channel Twelve weather report before we left. When you walk everywhere, you gotta keep an eye on the weather just like pilots do.

"Anyway, we thought it might be a fireworks display or a laser show, so we sat down to watch."

"Did you see me?" I asked.

"Not at first, but we saw someone who looked a lot like Tuwanda on the roof."

"Ain't no one who looks like Tuwanda except Tuwanda," murmured Tuwanda.

At least she was following the conversation. The drug couldn't have affected her too much.

"Then it was you on that roof?" Larry asked her.

"Damn straight."

Culpepper manically jingled the coins in his pocket.

"This is a waste of time. He's not telling us anything we didn't already know."

He emphasized each of the last three words with a coin jingle.

Larry straightened up and looked Culpepper in the eyes. "Haven't you ever heard of corroboration?"

Good one, I thought.

Culpepper rolled his eyes again but didn't say anything more about the subject.

"As I was saying before I was interrupted, Tuwanda was on the roof, and then there was another flash. Someone was hanging out of the window but then fell out of the window when an alien tried to pull him or her back into the building."

Everyone looked at me expectantly.

I shrugged and nodded. "That's consistent with Nelsen Nelsen Jr.'s version."

"Who?" interjected Les.

"Nelsen Nelsen Sr.'s son," I said. When Les continued to stare, I added, "The gentleman who was hung, or who hanged himself, in the bakery building."

"Was that you fallin' out of the window, Mom?" asked Larry.

"I guess it was. I don't remember anything after I saw the alien, who was really Nelsen Nelsen Jr."

"Someone ran out of the house about a minute before the alien did," continued Larry. "I knew it wasn't the alien, because it wasn't shiny. I didn't see where that person went, because then the alien came out, and I was distracted by what he did after that."

To speed things up, I summarized the rest of the story as told to me by Nelsen Jr. regarding what happened before I was conscious and as remembered by me afterward. When I finished, I asked Larry if he could remember anything about the person who had run out of the house before Nelsen Jr. did.

"Nope. Not really," he responded. "But Jacob did. He told me."

"Jacob, what did you see?" I asked.

"I saw a black Ford 150 with a short bed and lotsa chrome. It had those wide tires with deep tread, and the truck was set up maybe a foot between the tires and the wheel wells."

"How could you see all that at night?" Carter asked suspiciously.

"He stopped under a streetlight before taking off down the main road, heading north."

"He's right. I've been by there. It's the only streetlight in the neighborhood," I added. "Jacob, could you see who was in the car?"

"Nope, but whoever it was was a rude driver. He—or she, because women can be rude too—sped down that dirt road at about fifty miles an hour, throwin' all kinds of dust and dirt into the air. To be polite to the people livin' on either side of the road, you should drive slow."

We all nodded, and I decided I liked Jacob.

"What did you guys do once the alien and I left?" I asked.

"We walked to the factory and looked around; then Jacob called the FBI, of course," said Larry.

"The FBI? Why not the police?"

"Jacob here is an ex-marine. He's done six tours of duty in Iraq and a couple in Afghanistan. I always thought it was strange that they called them tours. Makes it sound like a vacation. Jacob, go ahead and tell 'em why you called the FBI."

Jacob straightened and saluted me.

I was a strange choice for that honor.

"Ma'am, at approximately twenty-two hundred hours, I inspected the premises surrounding the factory building. I noticed a saguaro cactus with a perfectly round hole burned through its middle. I followed what I thought might be the trajectory of whatever caused the hole and found the same type of hole, but higher, on a cactus nearer to the bakery. The shape and placement of the holes were like those of a laser.

"Lasers don't make sound, which was consistent with the noiseless blue flashes we saw. But you can't see laser beams without an infrared scope, and the ones I saw with the naked eye were blue. So I thought it might be an experimental laser. Scientists sometimes put colored mineral powder in the laser so they can see how and where it travels.

"If this was an experimental laser, the FBI needed to know about it. I did not have a phone, sir, so we had to hitchhike back to the shelter to call."

Carter picked up the story. "As soon as the FBI talked to Jason, they brought NSA in on the investigation."

"We did not bring NSA in on it," interjected Culpepper tersely. "You guys were wiretapping us."

"Big deal. We wiretap everyone, and so do you," Carter countered.

"By the time we got there, the air-force guys had dropped in," he continued. "Apropos of nothing, I wish NSA let us do a dramatic entrance once in a while. It's so damned cool. Anyway, we hung around for a while and listened to what the ninja warriors were saying. Culpepper and his guys were skulking around the perimeter."

"We saw her out there too," said Culpepper, jerking his head toward Tuwanda.

Carter ignored Culpepper's interruption and continued. "We drove to the Our Lady of the Bleeding Heart Shelter to find Larry and Jacob, but a fellow wearing a kilt and rain boots told us they'd gone on their scavenging rounds. It took us a whole day to find them."

"It was the day before garbage pickup. We had to move fast," said Larry.

"I've been grilling this guy for a day and a half," said Carter, pointing to Larry. "All he's said is that the aliens and zombies are coming and I should get an invisible coat before it's too late."

"What good's that gonna do?" slurred Tuwanda.

Culpepper and Carton twitched at the sound of her voice. They had forgotten about her.

"What you gotta get is somethin' that makes *you* invisible. Who gives a damn if the coat is invisible?"

Her logic was unassailable.

"So all's we know is that the unsub drives a tricked-up black Ford 150," she said.

I thought she'd fallen asleep, but she'd been listening the whole time.

"What's an unsub?" I asked.

All of them, even Larry and Jacob, answered in unison: "Unknown subject."

"The agents on *Criminal Minds* say it all the times," explained Larry, as if that helped.

"And don't forget the *Unsub* series with David Soul," said Jacob seriously.

"David Soul? Oh, man. I haven't heard that name in years," said Tuwanda.

"That's probably the same thing his agent thinks too," said Culpepper, laughing at his own joke.

I sensed that the discussion had gone off track.

"We now know what the *unsub* was driving. What else do we know?"

"That he or she worked for or with the government and had access to experimental lasers," said Jacob.

"Good. So we need to find out who has access to the laser."

"Plus who has the clearance to get on the base and steal it," said Culpepper.

"How do you mean?" asked Tuwanda.

"All civilian and military personnel with access to experimental or current weapons are checked at the gate coming and going and are thoroughly searched. Only folks with top clearance bypass the search process," explained Carter.

"So give us an example of who got top clearance," said Tuwanda.

"President Obama," said Jacob unhelpfully.

"I don't think Obama's got time to mess around with this shit. Anyone else?"

Jacob tried again. "The chairman of the Joint Chiefs of Staff."

"Again. We got skirmishes and technical advice goin' on. The chairman of the Joint Chiefs of Staff ain't gonna be crouchin' in no field with a laser."

"The janitorial staff," said Culpepper.

This made no sense to me. "The vice president of the United States doesn't have top clearance, but the janitor does?"

"Makes sense to me," said Carter. "Janitors actually do something."

"I don't know. Kerry works hard," said Larry.

Culpepper shook his head as if he were trying to clear his brain of Larry's comment.

"Yes, Secretary Kerry does work hard," he said slowly. "But we were talking about Biden."

"Who?"

The good ship *Unfocused* was drifting off course again.

"What if it wasn't a janitor but someone who stole a janitor's ID?" I suggested.

"All facilities dealing with sensitive matters require, at minimum, an eye scan to gain access," said Jacob.

"He's right," said Carter, looking at Jacob suspiciously.

"So we're back to the president, General Dempsey, and Bob's Janitorial or whatever its name is," I said.

"Or maybe one of them has an identical twin," added Larry.

"Shut up," said Culpepper.

"So what do we do now?" I asked him.

"*We* don't do anything. Our office will run a cross-check on everyone with access to experimental lasers that drives a black truck."

"Ford 150," corrected Larry.

"Seriously. Shut up.

"As I was about to say before I got interrupted, once we get the results of the cross-check, we'll go get our man—or woman."

"How long does the cross-check take?" I asked.

"Depends on how fast the hits come in. The system searches alphabetically."

"So if the dude's got a name like Zyger, then how long?" asked Tuwanda.

"An hour maybe."

"Let the NSA handle this one," said Carter. "Our equipment is newer and faster."

Culpepper glared at him. "Your funding is newer and faster."

"What the hell does that mean?" Carter spat back. "You know, you guys should really get over this funding thing."

"Fine," I interjected. "Carter, use the NSA equipment. Once we have the results of the search, then what do we do?"

"*We* do nothing. Carter and I take it from there," said Culpepper huffily. "By the way, why aren't you dead? The guys in autopsy want to take you apart to find out how you resurrected the first time. They're going to be real upset with this development."

I had been wondering when someone would get around to asking that.

"I was only resurrected once. I faked the second death," I said, which was partially true but largely not. "Wait a minute. Leslie, you knew I was lying in that room dead, and you felt nothing?"

"God, that's sick, Kate," he said.

"That's not what I meant, and you know it." I knew I wasn't going to get anywhere, though, so I let my righteous indignation fizzle out and moved on to another issue.

"Since I am one of the victims in this whole mess, you at least owe me an obligation to keep me posted on future developments."

"She's right," said Carter. "We're subject to federal and state victim's-rights statutes."

Culpepper just smiled, and I knew, statutory obligation notwithstanding, he wasn't going to tell me anything.

Carter would, though.

Culpepper and Carter closed their notebooks and moved to leave.

"Hey," said Tuwanda. "You gotta drive us home. I *know* you got transportation."

"Fair enough," said Culpepper. "Let me call the drivers who took you here."

"You'd better not," said Carter. Jerking his head toward Tuwanda, he said, "I'm pretty sure she will hurt them for kidnapping her. You'd better let me make the arrangements for another driver."

Culpepper grunted. Carter interpreted this response as a yes and went into his office, presumably to find us a driver.

"Hey. We need rides too," said Larry, indicating himself and Jacob.

Tuwanda snorted. "Not with us, you ain't. You smell."

Larry pointed to me. "So does *she*."

He was undoubtedly right, but still, I was hurt. "Well, you've got tinfoil on your head."

"We gotta set aside some time to work on your comebacks, Katie," said Tuwanda.

Carter jogged out of his office and announced that arrangements had been made. Our driver would pick up all of us at the front door of the building in a few minutes.

Carter led us to the front door, and as soon as we arrived, a horn sounded from outside.

Everyone piled in, with no room to spare. The driver asked that Tuwanda sit next to him, probably partly to provide an odor buffer and partly because she was gorgeous.

As we left, I looked back to see where the NSA, CIA, FBI, or whatever had held us. It was a diaper-cleaning operation.

Tuwanda insisted that I stay clear of my condo until whoever was trying to zap me was arrested. I pointed out that it was just as likely that someone was trying to zap her, but she brushed off my logic.

The driver first dropped Tuwanda and me off at Tuwanda's apartment and then headed downtown with Larry and Jacob.

"Shower and then bed," Tuwanda said as we rode the elevator to her floor.

"Shower, call client, and then bed," I countered.

Tuwanda made a face but said, "Done deal."

I took a long shower, luxuriating in the feeling of warm water and impending cleanliness. I let go of my thoughts and let them float where they might.

One thought was not into floating, however. It bumped against my consciousness like a balloon battered by the wind.

I focused more carefully on the annoying thought while I dried off.

If you take away the aliens, the laser, the army, and the NSA, CIA, and FBI, what is left is Nelsen Nelsen Sr.'s death. Was the laser and alien stuff intended to distract us from Nelsen Sr.'s murder? Tuwanda and I were searching the third floor of the abandoned bakery when the first laser hit. Maybe somebody didn't want us to find something, such as evidence relating to Nelsen Sr.'s death. What better way to clear out a building than zap it with a weapons-grade laser?

I found a writing tablet in Tuwanda's guest bedroom and jotted down this theory, labeling it as number one. Then I wrote, as item number two, *What if the object someone didn't want us to find was unrelated to Nelsen Sr.'s death and involved a perpetrator and motive we hadn't considered?*

Having preserved my thoughts in writing, my brain being an unreliable storage unit, I next called the Fourth Avenue jail, identified myself, and asked to speak to Deacon Davis.

What seemed like a long time elapsed before I heard Deacon Davis's voice.

"Hey, Miss Kate. Found anything yet?" he asked, sounding as if he didn't expect to hear anything encouraging.

I brought him up to date, leaving out the parts where I had died and US agents had kidnapped me, because I didn't think they were relevant to his arrest.

"Do you know of anything stored in the building that would be of value?" I asked.

"Nope. Just trash. Oh, and there's a bunch of old boxes in the third-floor storage room."

"Did you ever look in the boxes?"

"One of them is open, and it was just filled with files of spreadsheets, letters, memos, and such like. We left 'em alone because we figured they might be important to someone lookin' to start up the business again."

"How many boxes would you say there are?"

"Lots. More than fifty."

MJ, Sam, Beth, and I had a long search ahead of us, one that would require protective measures against paper cuts (gloves) and boredom (coffee).

I explained my theories to the deacon and outlined our next move. His only response was an unenthusiastic "Okay."

I went to bed after Tuwanda stuck her head in and yelled, "Sleep!" My brain wasn't copasetic with the plan, though. My body screamed exhaustion, but my neurons were convinced that work still needed to be done. I closed my eyes, but that just excited them more because the darkness helped eliminate distractions. My body eventually won, and I fell asleep. Stymied, my neurons turned to my dreams to express themselves. Unfortunately, dreams are a less-efficient medium than wide-awake brain cells.

I dreamed of aliens, pools, Ent-like trees, uncaring NSA agents, and black trucks. After I woke up, it took a while for the muddled mess to gel, and I realized I had forgotten to include my theory about Nelsen Sr. witnessing a murder involving a drowning in my house's backyard.

I jotted down theory number three, but it didn't seem promising. In fact, in my fully awakened state, I realized we had little evidence to support any of my theories. At this stage, everything was a riddle wrapped in a mystery inside an enigma. (My apologies to Winston Churchill for mangling his brilliant phraseology.) But that was the case with most of my ideas until I had a chance to flesh them out. My musings were interrupted by Tuwanda yelling that the coffee was on. That got me out of bed. Coffee is my lifeblood.

Once I was seated at the kitchen table with a huge mug of coffee cradled in my hands, I explained my three theories to Tuwanda.

When I finished, she reaffirmed my earlier conclusion. "I think the message is to keep an open mind and not commit to any theory, because we ain't got enough evidence to prove anything yet."

"I know," I said glumly.

"So what we gonna do next?"

"I'm going to corral MJ, Sam, and Beth into going with me to search the bakery's third-floor storage room."

"I been in that room. There's a lot of boxes to search in there. I gotta do inventory today at Pole Polishers, but once I'm through, I'll come over and give you a hand."

Tuwanda guessed what my raised eyebrows were about. "All our costumes, birth-control stuff, advertising signs and flyers, equipment, and such like."

This only prompted more questions, but I let it go.

"If you're not too tired, we'd appreciate your help," I said.

"Good. That's settled then. I'll see you around three."

"A.m. or p.m.?"

"P.m."

Thank God.

I contacted my staff and explained the plan. No one was thrilled with the assignment, but it beat sitting in the office. We convened at the old bakery at ten o'clock in the morning. Beth picked me up on her way, because my balance was still iffy.

The bakery was sealed with yellow police tape, army green tape, red tape (FBI), black tape (CIA?), and fluorescent pink tape (NSA?). It looked like an attempt at making the world's largest twine ball. Cawker City had nothing to worry about, though.

"I don't think we can go through that tape," said Beth. "It's illegal."

MJ snorted.

"God, MJ," shrilled Sam. "Every time you snort—and you do it a lot—snot sprays out. I'm probably breathing in snot particles."

MJ ignored him. "Kate's gone through police tape before."

"Only once," I protested. "And that was because it was blocking the door to my office."

"How about we do this?" said Sam. "Kate, you break the police tape since you have some experience with that. MJ, you take the FBI tape because it's only a matter of time before they arrest you for something anyway. I'll take the black tape, and, Beth, you take the hot pink tape."

"Where should we start cutting?" asked MJ.

"I vote for the tape sealing the front door," said a voice behind us.

Crap. Bryan, Mr. Law and Order, was standing behind us, looking every inch the conservatives' wet dream for sheriff. His dirty-blond hair, streaked silver gray since I met him, was combed smooth with a side part. I knew for a fact that he had soft little curls at the nape of his neck that were screaming to be free. His blue eyes were covered by aviator sunglasses, and his six-feet, two-inch frame was ensconced in a politically correct, not-too-expensive, not-too-cheap navy suit, white shirt, and red tie. He reminded me of James Bond (à la Pierce Brosnan).

"Why don't you stick your bureaucratic nose out and cut the tapes?" chided MJ.

"I will supervise," he said, picking his way through the detritus toward us.

"Good enough for me," I said. Under an agency theory, Bryan would be liable for all of us.

"Let's get this ribbon-cuttin' ceremony started," called out Tuwanda as she zigzagged among rocks, weeds, and trash.

"I thought you weren't coming until later," I said.

"I din't wanta miss anythin'. By the way, I drove by your condo as your mother and Jane was walkin' into your buildin'. They was wearin' tennis clothes. Your mom looked pretty good, but that Jane ain't built for tiny skirts and tight tops."

Just as well, I thought. *If Mom were here, she'd tsk so much she'd wear out her tsker.*

"Let's do this, guys. Today," ordered Bryan.

Beth pulled scissors out of her purse and handed them to Bryan. Beth would have made a great Eagle Scout.

Bryan made short work out of cutting the tape.

I was the first to try the door. "It's locked," I said.

MJ came up next to me and gently nudged me aside. She then took something out of her purse and motorcycle tool kit, which was pink leather with red hearts, and jiggled it around in the keyhole. The door swung open.

Bryan looked at me sharply.

I shrugged.

"I don't want to know," said Bryan.

Bryan asked everyone to fall in behind him while he took the lead.

Right. We do all the work, and he does the macho-cop fun part.

Only it wasn't fun.

CHAPTER 27

A man dressed in karate clothes stood in the doorway. Unfortunately, his flabby chest and potbelly ruined the whole ninja-warrior effect. He wore a ski mask, so we couldn't tell who he was.

I then noticed he had a gun trained on us, which added points to the ninja look.

Rather than shoot us, he took an action that I, and likely my companions as well, thought was wise and humanitarian. He walked out of the house and down the path. When he got to the road, he turned and ran like hell. Somewhere in the darkness, a car started and then took off in the direction opposite the main road.

"Who was that masked man?" asked Beth. Her attempted humor was belied by her trembling voice.

"Did anyone notice if he was carrying anything?" asked Bryan.

"Yeah. A gun," said Tuwanda.

"Other than the gun," clarified Bryan.

"I was kinda distracted by the gun, so I din't notice," said Tuwanda.

We all nodded in agreement.

"Tuwanda and Kate, once we're inside, please point out anything different from what you saw when you were here before," said Bryan.

"First off, there was that fat ninja," said Tuwanda.

"Duly noted," Bryan responded.

We lined up behind Bryan again and followed him into the house. Since his status had changed from that of line leader to that of shield, I didn't mind that he was up front.

"The trash has been raked," I commented.

"The police did that," Bryan said. "FYI, they didn't find anything relevant to lasers or Nelsen's death, but they're still talking about the stuff they did find. One officer had to be sent home sick. Another was convinced he'd gotten chlamydia from an old condom."

Tuwanda made a disgusted sound. "What the hell did he do with that nasty condom?"

There was a group shiver.

We climbed the stairs to the third floor. I didn't bother to point out the footprints left by the investigating officers.

The room where Nelsen died was crisscrossed with string attached to tacks. One of the strings led down the hall in the direction Tuwanda and I had run.

Tuwanda took the lead, and being careful not to disturb the strings, we followed her to a spot midway down the hall.

She squinted as she searched the wall. "There's no door."

Tuwanda ran her figure along the wall, and a thin gap appeared.

"Anybody got a screwdriver?" she asked.

Beth pushed her way to the front of the line and pulled both a Phillips and a flat head out of her purse.

Bryan chose the flat-head screwdriver. "I finally found someone with more stuff in her purse than you, Kate."

Losing that distinction did not bother me.

Bryan used the screwdriver to trace the edges of a low door.

"Ralph's doggy door is bigger than that," I commented.

MJ snorted. "Ralph's doggy door is bigger than the entrance to St. Patrick's Cathedral."

Bryan stooped to examine the door and then pushed on its right side. The door popped open.

"It's open, but it's still small," said Beth, glancing down at her ample figure.

"I din't have no problem gettin' in and out," said Tuwanda unhelpfully.

"Thank you for your input, Little Miss Size Two," growled MJ.

"Actually, I think it's big enough for all of us to get through," I said. "Of course, not together."

"I'm up for trying, except MJ has to be last," said Sam.

"Why? Do you think I'll get stuck and hold up the show?" huffed MJ.

"The *show* is what I'm worried about," said Sam.

MJ looked at me questioningly.

"I think he means that you are wearing a very short skirt."

"Oh, for God's sake, Sam," intoned MJ. "You're gay. What's it matter to you?"

"It's not a matter of attraction. It's part of a universal desire to avoid having your nose shoved up someone's butt."

MJ decided to take the high road. "I'm going to forgive you since the matter is outside your realm of understanding, so you have no idea what you're talking about," she said with a toss of her head.

We got down to business, and amazingly, we all made it through the door, except Beth, who said she would stay outside and guard the entrance.

Once inside, Bryan took a small flashlight out of his pocket, perched it on a centrally located stack of boxes, and turned it on. For such a little thing, it threw off a lot of light.

The room was impressive in neither size nor furnishings. An old wooden desk and a captain's chair were situated in the middle of the room, and lots of boxes and dust covered the balance of the room. We couldn't move without stirring up a Depression-era dust bowl.

"Everyone, take a stack of boxes and go through them," ordered Bryan, back in commander-in-chief mode.

"No," said Tuwanda.

"No nos," said Bryan, looking us in the eyes to forestall a mutinous attack.

"Why don't you want to help search?" I asked.

"Cuz the thrill is gone. I din't mind lookin' for you an' the aliens an' then smugglin' you out of the hospital. I din't even mind the ninja. But this here's borin'. There's no challenge to it."

"It's possible we might find something really valuable in one of these boxes, like gold bullion," I pointed out, exaggerating slightly.

"You think so?"

I nodded.

"Then hell, let's get at it."

An hour later, I had finished searching the top three boxes in my stack. Tuwanda's original characterization of the work was dead-on.

I had found bookkeeping journals going back to 1983 and had made it through 1992 with nothing to show for it except a good grasp of bakery-business economics.

The journal for 1993 proved to be different. It fell open to pages of odd-looking thousand-dollar bills. The bills had all been issued in 1890. In total, they had a face value of $13,000—a fair amount but not enough to kill someone over.

Perhaps their worth went beyond face value.

"Is anyone here a numismatic?"

"Gesundheit," said Tuwanda.

"What's that what you said? It sounds dirty," said MJ.

Everyone agreed.

"Let me rephrase. Does anyone here collect cash and coins?"

Everyone said yes.

I groaned. "This isn't working."

"A numismatic is someone who collects rare coins and cash for resale at a profit," said Bryan.

"I collect any kinda money," said Tuwanda, trying to grasp the distinction.

"So they sell a dollar for, like, a dollar fifty? You'd think people would see through that," said MJ.

Now they were just pulling my chain.

"What did you find, Kate?" asked Sam.

Thank God someone was staying on task.

"A bunch of thousand-dollar bills issued in 1890."

Sam pulled out his smartphone and punched out a search term.

"My God," he said excitedly. "Do they have a red seal on them?"

"Yes."

"What you've got there, if they're real, are grand watermelon thousand-dollar bills. One sold at auction a couple years ago for two million two hundred and twenty-five thousand dollars. How many did you say you have?"

"Thirteen."

Tuwanda, the quickest at math in our group due to her business experience, said, "Tha's twenty-eight million nine hundred and twenty-five thousand dollars."

We all let that sink in.

"Thank you," said a voice coming from the ceiling.

"Did the ceiling just say something?" asked MJ.

A trapdoor in the ceiling, the same one Tuwanda had lowered herself through the night of my disappearance, opened, and Nelsen Jr.'s face appeared. The top of his ninja suit was visible.

Then Ron's face appeared next to his.

Thinking of nothing better to say, I said, "Hi."

Bryan was on the ball. "What are you doing here?"

"We were going to search for the watermelons," said Ron, "but you did the work for us."

"*These* are what you were looking for the other night?" I asked. It was as close to a rhetorical question as you can get without asking a rhetorical question.

"Forget about the cash," said Bryan in his cop voice. "It's evidence now."

"Not really," said Ron calmly as he pointed a nine millimeter through the trapdoor.

He started firing. It was like shooting fish in a barrel.

He shot in Bryan's direction first, but Bryan had already taken cover against a wall behind piles of boxes and had pulled me with him.

He took aim at MJ next and would have killed her had Sam not jumped on top of her. Sam took a bullet in his back instead. Ron pointed the gun at Tuwanda, and she hit him with a barrage of books, tightly bound reams of paper, and jelly jars. I had no idea why the jars were there.

Ron yelped and withdrew the gun. (Nelsen Jr.'s head had disappeared as soon as the shooting started.)

"You the ones that killed Nelsen Sr.," accused Tuwanda, still throwing anything she could get her hands on at him. Bryan and I joined Tuwanda in her throwing strategy.

I glanced at MJ and Sam to see how they were doing.

MJ had crawled out from under Sam and was tugging him toward the door. Sam's body was unresponsive, and he didn't make a sound.

Ron broke into laughter. "You'd think we killed Nelsen Sr. in light of the present circumstances. But in fact, we did not. Our only interest has always been to find the watermelon bills. When he wouldn't tell Nelsen Jr.—"

"Just Nelsen, thank you," corrected Nelsen Jr.

"Where the bills were, we left him here. The murderer must have arrived as soon as we left. Kind of around the time you showed up, Kate."

"Kate did *not* kill Nelsen," huffed Tuwanda. "By the way, when we referrin' to the deceased Mr. Nelsen, should we still refer to 'im as Nelsen Sr.? If we gotta call 'em both Nelsen now, it's gonna get real confusin' real fast."

"If you didn't kill Nelsen, um, the deceased, then why ruin a perfectly good record of nonmurder by killing us?" I asked.

"Because you would tell everyone what you'd found, and instead of Nelsen—the live one—and me splitting the money, his sister would get half, and each of us would only get half of half. You see the problem."

MJ was backing out the door, dragging Sam along with her. Bryan motioned for Tuwanda and me to follow them.

Tuwanda went to the door and dropped to her knees, getting in line behind the other two. She helped MJ by shoving Sam's limp body ahead of her.

Something made me hesitate, though. I couldn't leave Bryan to a face a certain death.

Bryan jerked his head toward the door, and I shook my head.

"You love me," he mouthed.

I considered tossing something at his head, but we were running out of ammunition.

Ron aimed the gun at me again, and again, Bryan shoved me out of the way.

Ron grunted in exasperation. "Stay still."

"We have a lookout outside the door, and she's probably called the police," I said, trying again.

Ron's response was blunt: "She's dead."

We heard scuffling on the roof.

A cop voice said, "Drop your gun or you're dead."

It sounded like Officer Jeff Bridges.

We heard a thud. Ron might have been a desperate man, but he wasn't stupid.

I collapsed against Bryan.

CHAPTER 28

I came to at my old stomping grounds, the hospital.

"I guess the good news is that you didn't die again," said the doctor who'd seen me before. His face was looming above mine as he peered into my eyes with an ophthalmoscope. "Your new concussion is doing great."

What did that mean? That my concussion had found a good job and bought a condo?

"I'm concerned about your peripheral vision, though."

"How's Sam?" There was nothing wrong with my memory.

The doctor lowered the ophthalmoscope and sat back. His features settled into a serious but concerned expression. He probably had to practice it a lot because the concerned part in particular did not come naturally to him.

"I'm afraid your friend has passed on."

My mind froze, my mouth went dry, and my ears started to ring.

"Please repeat what you just said," I croaked.

"Your friend passed on," he repeated obligingly.

The words sounded the same as the first time he had said them.

"There's a gentleman waiting for you in the lobby. There were two gentlemen, but we had to tell one of them to leave, because the two of them were bare-knuckle fighting. Should I get the one who's still there?"

Panic had bled into his voice. Consolation was not part of his verbal or emotional repertoire.

I nodded numbly.

He scuttled out of the room, and in under a minute, Bryan was standing next to my bed.

"That bastard told you, didn't he? Dammit. I told him to call me in when you woke up."

"Sam—dead?" My brain unfroze, and then my tears flowed out like water from a broken hydrant.

Bryan nodded and held my hand.

"Beth too?"

"She's got a nasty shoulder wound, but otherwise, she's doing fine. She said she played dead once Ron shot her. As soon as Nelsen Jr. and Ron left, Beth called 911 on her cell. She saved our lives."

"Not Sam's."

My tears had soaked the pillow, so Bryan left to get another one.

While he was gone, a heartening but weird thought occurred to me: *What if Sam is dead like I was dead and will hang out in limbo before the weird-looking guy pushes him into the hole?*

It was a slim hope, but it was something.

Bryan returned with a fresh pillow, mumbling about the lack of humanity in hospitals. While he switched out my pillow, he told me about his quest for what was apparently the holy grail of hospital wards. He'd finally found someone willing to find him a fresh pillow. The Good Samaritan was another patient who'd been there for over a week and had learned the ropes.

Once the pillow switch was accomplished, Bryan straightened up and looked at me intently.

"You've stopped crying, and you look kind of happy. Are you okay? Should I call the doctor?"

"No. I'm fine," I insisted.

Bryan continued to scrutinize my face. "You're hoping Sam will resurrect, aren't you?"

I nodded and did not meet his eyes.

He started to say something but then clamped his mouth shut, smiled slightly, and patted my hand.

Condescending asshole, I thought.

Something else occurred to me. "Did Ron and Nelsen Jr. admit to killing Nelsen Sr. yet?"

"No, and the Phoenix Police Department and county sheriff's offices dug deep and long. Both their alibis held up."

"Did you talk to that boy I tol' you about?" asked a voice from the door.

"Come on in, Tuwanda. Kate's conscious."

"What boy?" I asked.

"While I was canvassin' my ole stompin' grounds, lookin' for witnesses, I found this li'l nine-year-old kid home alone who said he'd spotted an alien. I get the feelin' he spotted somethin' else, too. He said he had to quit lookin' at whatever it was, cuz his mom called him home. But if this kid was anythin' like I was at his age, he did no such thing. He woulda hung out until his mama's voice got screechy and she started makin' death threats. That'd give him a good five minutes more."

"Where is this kid?" asked Bryan. "I can have my office follow up a.s.a.p."

"First, his name's Jevon, and he's at 2405 East Paradise Drive, which is ironic cuz it's far from paradise. It's more like a heav'ly armed third-world country. Most importantly for your purposes, they don't trust law enforcement at all. Law enforcement only shows up in their neighborhoods to arrest someone."

"Even the sheriff's department?" asked Bryan, sounding genuinely surprised.

"Especially the sheriff's department. Your guys think it's still the Wild West out here, an' if you black or brown, the rules don't apply."

"I have to fix that," said Bryan.

"Well, don't say nothin' about that while you're running. You'd lose for sure. Only conservative old white people vote in this state. Everyone else has given up. They say the last liberal moved to Florida last week. Florida! Can you imagine that? He's thinkin' Florida is more progressive, and tha's a state where the legislature is still tryin' to figure out how to repeal the Thirteenth Amendment and the Civil Rights Act of 1964."

"Do you want to drive out with me then and smooth the way?" asked Bryan.

Both Tuwanda and I said, "Yes!"

"Kate, you can't go. You haven't been discharged from the hospital," pointed out Bryan.

"That don't stop her. Katie, get your clothes on."

"I'm not sure I should. I've heard from several people that my ensemble stinks—literally."

Bryan went to a white metal cupboard and pulled out a plastic bag. "I brought you clean clothes from your apartment," he said, tossing the bag onto the bed. "I'll wait for you in the lobby."

As soon as he left, I grabbed the bag and went through its contents.

"Heels, Victoria's Secret underwear, and a silk St. John's dress? What was he thinking of?"

"He wasn't thinkin'. He was *wishful* thinkin'. Deep down inside, every man wants his woman to look like a fragile li'l flower, which is what you'll be, because you can't do shit in silk and heels."

Since I didn't have any other options, I put on the delicate-flower ensemble.

Tuwanda and I strode confidently out to the lobby. Tuwanda's strongly held belief is that appearance has nothing to do with anything. It's all attitude. If you walk into a room you just left with an entirely different attitude, no one will recognize you. Since I was comatose when I arrived, this would be a piece of cake.

When Bryan saw me, he gave a low whistle and fell in behind us.

We quickened our step once we were outside and headed for the parking garage. A hand shot out of an agave, and Bryan disappeared.

Tuwanda and I followed the sound of scuffling around to the back of the agave.

Mark and Bryan were going at each other—hard.

With surprising strength on our parts, Tuwanda and I dragged the two apart. I took Bryan because he was smaller.

"I would've beat up that bastard before if he hadn't played the sheriff card," growled Mark, pointing a shaking finger at Bryan.

"Look what you've done. Kate is in a frail condition, and you're putting her through all this shit," said Bryan.

I was not frail. *Damn dress and heels.*

Mark shook loose from Tuwanda, straightened, brushed off his pants, and said, "I love you, Kate."

Nobody said anything, but Bryan was making animal noises, as if he were building up to another attack. I got a better grip on his arms.

"Well, this is awkward," said Tuwanda. "Maybe you an' Kate should wait until you're alone to have that kinda talk."

"They'll be alone over my dead body," Bryan spat out.

"Come on, guys. We've got to get moving on this, or we'll lose our window of opportunity." I had no idea if this was true, but it seemed to work. Both men relaxed a bit.

"Where are you going?" asked Mark.

"We goin' to South Phoenix to interview a nine-year-old kid."

"I'll go with you," said Mark.

"Okay," said Tuwanda.

Flaming arrows shot out of Bryan's eyes.

Tuwanda ignored him. "C'mon then. We gotta leave."

"I'll sit in the back with Kate," said Mark.

"You'll ride in the front with me," said Bryan.

Tuwanda and I agreed that Bryan's suggestion was probably the better of the two.

When we got to Tuwanda's car, we scrambled into our assigned seats, with Bryan at the wheel.

The front-seat occupants were surprisingly civil throughout the ride. There were no outbreaks of violence, only constant streams of muttering from which I could make out the occasional word or phrase, such as "steroid monkey," "concave-chested asshole," and something about one of them needing a bra.

As we neared South Twenty-Fourth Street, Tuwanda snaked her hand between the two front seats and fiddled with the dials on the radio. A rap song came on, and Tuwanda twirled up the volume to an unbearably loud setting.

Covering my ears with my hands, I yelled, "Won't the music draw attention to us?"

"No!" shouted Tuwanda. "But not havin' the music will. This here's the Booty Boys an' their latest hit, 'I'm Gonna Get Dirty Wit' You, Girl, so Bring Antibacterial Wipes.'"

"That's a long title," I yelled.

"It includes all the lyrics. I guess it's so people can read the title an' sing along."

I nodded as if I understood, but I didn't.

Bryan pulled up to the address Tuwanda had given him. The daylight brought the littered front yards, sagging gates, and peeling paint of the houses in the neighborhood into full focus. Jevon's duplex looked uninhabitable.

Tuwanda told us to wait in the car until she got permission for us to enter. Then she disappeared around the edge of the house and into the backyard.

A few minutes later, she motioned for us to come over.

When we rounded the corner of the house, I spotted a small boy sitting on a battered lawn chair that used to be white but was now—is *yuck* a color?

He stood up as soon as he saw me, and he gestured for me to take the chair. Since it was the only chair in the yard, I couldn't refuse the honor, so I sat down. It was sticky in places—lots of places—so my flowing dress would need to be dry-cleaned later.

"Jevon's gonna tell us what else he saw the night the alien, a.k.a. Nelsen Jr., kidnapped Kate here—aren't cha, Jevon?"

"I want half up front," said Jevon, looking at Bryan suspiciously.

Tuwanda handed him a five-dollar bill.

He shoved it in the back pocket of his jeans.

"Okay. You can ask your questions. Except him." Jevon pointed at Bryan. "He's a cop. I can smell cops."

"Actually, I'm a sher—"

"Okay." I interrupted Bryan before he could recite his résumé. "We'll take turns asking questions, except for Bryan—the one who smells like a cop."

"What does a cop smell like?" asked Mark.

"An asshole," Jevon answered promptly.

Mark laughed so hard that I thought he would make himself sick. His face turned bright red, and he had to gasp for breath.

"God, I love this kid," he wheezed.

Bryan moved next to Mark.

Mark looked surprised and then yelled, "Oh God," and doubled over.

I didn't see exactly what Bryan did, but I did see his hand shoot out and make a karate-chop motion.

Tuwanda shook her head and tsk-tsked. "I'm gonna ask the first question since these boys is playin' aroun' and not takin' any of this at all serious.

"Now, Jevon, you tol' me about the alien, an' I appreciate that. Did you see anythin' *after* you saw the alien?"

"I tol' you. My momma called, and I had to go home."

"I 'member when I was your age, I let my momma call a few times before I headed home. You know, so she din't develop unrealistic expectations. An' if I saw somethin' as cool as an alien, no way was I gonna scamper home right away."

Jevon stared down and scraped the bare ground with the toe of his tennis shoe.

"I'm feelin' kinda shy," he said. "Like I don't want to talk no more."

"I ain't givin' you no more money, Jevon. Jus' answer my questions, an' tell the truth."

Jevon kept looking down but stopped toeing the dirt. "You still owe me five dollars," he mumbled.

"Not till you answer my questions."

Jevon looked up defiantly. He didn't focus on any one of us, so it wasn't clear whether his defiance was directed at us or someone—or something—else.

"I saw a white man gettin' out of a tricked-up black truck that pulled up after the alien went into the old bakery. He stopped and looked around like he thought someone was watchin' him. When he saw me, he come over and picked me up by the front of my shirt. He got his face real close to mine an' said that if I tol' anyone I saw him there, he'd kill me an' my mamma."

"We're going to make sure he doesn't follow through on that threat," intoned Bryan.

Jevon sneered at him. "I din't know shit could talk."

Mark, who had recovered enough to stand up straight, started to laugh again. Experience had taught him nothing. Bryan shot to his side. Mark dodged the karate chop, but the karate kick hit its mark.

With Mark out of commission again, we turned back to Jevon.

"Can you describe the man?" I asked.

"Old. Maybe in his forties."

Three of the four adults present clenched their jaws.

"He was white an' got gray hair with a little black tip runnin' down the middle, kinda like a negative of Pepé Le Pew."

"Good simile," I said.

"My teacher says I'm good at similes too but that I gotta quit usin' swear words in 'em."

"What else do you remember about him?"

"He was tall, maybe six feet, an' he had a beer belly. He was wearin' a white-and-green team shirt."

"Which team's colors are white and green?" I asked.

"The Colts? The Jets in an away game?" ventured Mark between gasps.

"Shut up," said Bryan.

Jevon shook his head slowly. "No, it was a high school, cuz it had *HS* after the name. I think the name started with an *A*, but I'm not sure. That's as much as I can remember."

"You done good, Jevon," said Tuwanda kindly as she handed him another five-dollar bill.

We added our thanks to those of Tuwanda, and I extended an invitation to Jevon to join us for a celebratory dinner when we caught the bad guy.

"You have to ask your mom first, though," I added. "By the way, is she inside? I want to thank her for letting us borrow you."

Jevon shook his head. "No. She gone for a while."

"How long?" asked Tuwanda.

"It's different each time but usually a week or so. She's got to work to pay for our house an' food an' stuff."

Tuwanda placed her hands on his shoulders and knelt down until they were eye to eye. "Jevon, I want you to promise me that you'll go to the Pioneer Presbyterian Church an' find Reverend Booker. Tell him your situation, an' he'll find a place for you to stay till your momma gets back."

We took our assigned places in the car, and as soon as Bryan got to the main road, Tuwanda called Reverend Booker and explained Jevon's situation. When she hung up, she told us the reverend was going to go to Jevon's house to pick him up.

That was good news, because I doubted Jevon would have sought out the reverend.

"By the way, I forgot to tell you," said Bryan. "Deacon Davis's case was continued when you died. Plus, someone posted his bail, and he's out on his own recognizance."

Bryan looked at me meaningfully. I looked away.

I leaned back on the car's comfy pink leather and closed my eyes. Letting my thoughts float, twirl, and collide sometimes helped me figure things out.

"Does anyone know of someone who fits Jevon's description of the bad guy?" asked Bryan.

"Shh," admonished Tuwanda. "Kate's lettin' her thoughts float, twirl, an' collide."

The occupants of the car fell silent out of either respect or confusion.

The slight rocking of the car was lulling me to sleep until Bryan made a hard left and interrupted the lulling. My happy, sleepy brain cells were rudely awakened when they smashed against one another and then ricocheted off in multiple directions, looking for other cells to smash into out of spite.

"Could the shirt worn by the man Jevon saw have said Arcadia High School? A family with a teenage son lives across the street from the house I'm buying. He was wearing a shirt like the one Jevon described on the first day I saw him."

Then another thought hit me. I was on a roll.

"And he drives a tripped-out black truck."

"But he's not an old man in his forties, and I'm guessing he doesn't have a potbelly," said Bryan.

Both were good points, but Bryan couldn't use them to shoot down my theory. I could explain the discrepancy. "It might have been his father."

"Okay, but please explain what possible motive the father had to kill Nelsen Sr."

"Because Nelsen was in his tree the night of the pool party in my house's backyard—the night Tiffany Jacobs drowned."

Bryan rolled his eyes. "You're buying a house where a person died? Why does this not surprise me?"

Tuwanda slapped Bryan's arm. "Ignore him, Kate. I'm puttin' him on jerk status and shovin' him to the back of my brain. You should do the same.

"I get what you sayin', Kate. You sayin' that kid across the street either killed or maybe coulda saved that young girl, an' his dad wanted to get rid of the one witness who could destroy his son's future."

Even Bryan looked impressed—but not for long.

"So why'd he wait a year to kill Nelsen Sr.?" asked Bryan, unphased by his jerk status.

"I'm hearin' this li'l squeaky voice in the back of my brain, but I can't make out what it's sayin'," said Tuwanda. "It sounded kinda like a jerk talkin'."

I wasn't going to play along, because I'd suddenly realized why Nelsen had been murdered.

"He killed Nelsen because of me," I said.

CHAPTER 29

They waited for me to continue.

"He and I talked," I said, "and he made sense. He was no longer the crazy man in the tree whose testimony couldn't be trusted. I could vouch for that. So they killed him."

"So where do this man and his family live?" asked Bryan.

Because he hadn't said anything sarcastic, I thought maybe he kind of accepted my logic.

Tuwanda gave him the address of my future home, explaining, "Tha's the address of where Katie gonna live. The man we lookin' for lives across the street."

Bryan made a hard right, undoing the hard left he'd just made, and we headed in the direction of Arcadia.

"I had no idea you were moving," said Mark.

"If it makes you feel any better, I didn't know either," said Bryan. "Do you think she's trying to get away from us by not telling us where she's going to live?"

I made an exasperated sound. "Don't be sulky little boys. No one knew except Tuwanda, and that's because she went house hunting with me. I didn't think I'd find a house so fast."

"I met your real-estate agent, Jane, the night you went missing, Kate," commented Bryan. "I figured she was a friend of your mother's, because they stuck together like glue. She kept hitting on me."

"My *mother?*"

"No. Jane."

"She kept hitting on me, too," said Mark.

Bryan snorted. "You're just saying that because you don't want anyone to think you're less attractive than me."

"Really? Then why did she give me her address and put her house key in my pocket?"

Mark produced a key attached to a Swarovski-encrusted gold dollar sign.

"That could be anyone's," he shot back.

Bryan didn't sound that confident, though. I think even he recognized his logic was weak.

"Jane's a jerk for flirting with my men," I said, "but I forgive her because she kept my mother busy."

"You've never introduced me to your mother," said Bryan.

"Me either," said Mark.

Little did they know that my omissions had saved their souls.

We arrived at my future house, having agreed en route that we would avoid suspicion by pretending to be prospective purchasers—or, in my case, a real purchaser—when in fact, we would be taking turns watching the house across the street. If we saw no sign of life in thirty minutes, we would sashay over and break into the garage.

The sun was low in the sky, and we were going to lose the light soon. Each of us felt a sense of urgency.

Tuwanda took the first watch while I showed Mark and Bryan the house—a tour that consisted of walking around the yard and peering into the windows. Both pronounced the home "really nice" and complimented me on my good taste.

The two men joined Tuwanda at her post, and I wandered around the backyard, inevitably ending up under Nelsen's tree. I peered up into its branches in the failing light and wondered if it missed Nelsen. Maybe it was glad he was gone so that its branches wouldn't have to hold his weight anymore. I liked to think the former was the case, because it seemed like a nice tree.

A dark blob crossed my line of vision, startling me. The blob disappeared as quickly as it had come, though, and I chided myself for being upset about what was probably a cat—a really big cat.

Something heavy glanced off the side my head.

I was able to stay on my feet, one of which I used to prod the side of the dark mass lying on the ground.

"Stop it, you bitch. That's my dick!"

Now that I realized that the mass was a foul-mouthed jerk, the field narrowed.

"Chad? What were you doing in the tree?" I asked.

"None of your goddamn business."

"Were you thinking about the girl you drowned? Criminals always return to the scene of the crime, you know."

"Fuck you," he responded with feeling.

Chad sprang to his feet, and I remembered how tall he was. I liked it better when he was curled up on the ground.

Another dark shape approached quickly from the side gate.

"Bryan?" I hazarded a hopeful guess.

"Kevin," corrected the shape.

The two of them moved toward me. I backed up at the same speed that they walked toward me until my back was against the block wall.

"Why did you ask my son about Tiffany?" Kevin asked, taking a step forward.

A weapon—at least I think it was a weapon—dangled from his right hand. It looked like a pregnant rifle.

My intelligent brain cells were apparently the only ones injured by the series of concussions I'd suffered over the past couple of days, because they sat this one out and let the stupid, crazy, impulsive brain cells take over for the last quarter of play.

"Because I believe he drowned Tiffany, either by accident or on purpose, and you killed Nelsen because Nelsen saw the whole thing. Is that a laser gun you're holding?"

"You're crazy, lady," said Chad.

"You're dead, lady," said his dad.

"What do you think?" he asked his son. "She falls, hits her head, and then drowns in the pool? Simple but effective, with a poetic symmetry."

"I'd like to hear from Chad before we make any decisions," I said, preferring Chad's characterization of me as crazy to his father's characterization of me as dead.

"Why don't you use your laser gun?" asked Chad, jerking his head toward the pregnant rifle. Then he said with a note of pride, "My dad works at Luke Air Force Base. He ripped the laser off from the development lab."

"I was right," I said under my breath.

Kevin made an exasperated noise. "I can't use it, because like everything made by the armed services, it's a piece of shit. It's broken. The laser's out. Any other suggestions?"

"I can drown her and *then* bash her head in so it looks like she fell and hit her head. That's what I did to Tiffany," offered Chad. "It'd be easier for me cuz I've already done it once before."

"God, you're stupid," said Kevin.

I figured all I needed to do was stall until my friends came looking for me. I prayed that Bryan had found a gun after our experience with Nelsen Jr. and Ron at the bakery. A gun would trump the rock Kevin was picking up from the river-rock border encircling the flowers on the patio.

"Grab her," he ordered Chad.

"Where?" God had given Chad big muscles but had balanced the scales by making his brain small.

"I'll do it, shit for brains. Take the rock," Kevin said through his teeth.

One of my intelligent brain cells (an IBC) staggered to its feet and kicked one of the stupid, lazy ones (an SLC) in the head.

Dammit. Just tell her to scream! yelled the IBC, after which it collapsed and fell on top of the other IBCs.

The SLC rubbed its tiny, pointed cell head but had the wherewithal to order me to scream before it became distracted by a memory of me eating an ice-cream cone.

I screamed—loud and long. It was not like a "There's a spider the size of a MINI Cooper in the tub!" scream but an "Oh my God, aren't those the four horsemen of the apocalypse?" scream.

Chad panicked and froze. Kevin, proving there was indeed a hereditary link between father and son, said, "Shut up."

As if that was going to stop me.

"No one can hear you scream anyway, lady," he added, trying to explain his logic.

He dropped his defunct laser gun and grabbed the rock from Chad. He raised it above his head like Moses holding the tablets and then brought it down hard.

I moved my head, and my shoulder took the brunt of the blow. Kevin raised the rock again.

The cavalry galloped into the backyard, Bryan in front with his gun drawn and Mark following closely behind, brandishing his cell phone. I later found out he wasn't planning to use the phone as a weapon—his phone did not have a weapons app—but had called 911 and was shouting information as he ran.

Kevin and Chad didn't go down without a struggle. Chad threw his weight against Bryan and knocked the gun out of his hand. Mark tackled Chad and Bryan, the former for obvious reasons and the latter because he wanted to. They all fell to the ground and melded into an undifferentiated mass of arms and legs.

Kevin went for the gun, but I got there first. I held it in front of me as I'd seen TV detectives do.

"Stop or I'll shoot." I realized how trite this statement was as soon as I said it. "Don't come any closer, or I'll shoot your dick off and use it for a condiment."

Mark and Bryan, who had gotten Chad under control, appeared confused. All four men looked at one another and mouthed, "Condiment?"

Kevin dropped to the ground and put his hands on his head. Tuwanda moved to him quickly and bound his wrists and ankles with zip-tie handcuffs. (She always carried them with her. I think they were work related.)

She threw some handcuffs to Bryan, and Chad was likewise trussed up.

Sirens and then running footsteps sounded from the front drive.

"What kind of condiment?" asked Kevin.

Everyone looked at me expectantly.

I shrugged. "Meatballs?"

"That's not a condiment," said Mark.

The other guys grunted in agreement.

I tried again. "Relish?"

"That's just sick," said Mark.

I was saved from having to strain my SLCs for a better answer—my IBCs were still benched—when the police ran up and took charge of Kevin and Chad.

CHAPTER 30

SAM

I didn't know what place this was, but soft light glowed everywhere. I felt wonderful. I hadn't felt that good since—actually, I'd never felt that good.

People's shadows were moving about. There were no people attached to them, just shadows with human shapes. I looked down at what should have been me, and I was a shadow too.

I couldn't remember anything. I had no past. There was only the present. My future was a nonissue since I would have no way knowing what it was until it became the present.

I didn't care. I just wanted to keep feeling the way I did.

A nonshadow appeared and moved toward me. It was strange looking yet somehow familiar. Its tentacles moved slowly as if it were walking underwater.

I wasn't afraid of the nonshadow. I felt comforted by it.

It came closer, gently wrapped its tentacles around me, and held me like a mother holds a baby. It led me to a whirling vortex and pushed me into the blackness.

The next thing I remembered was a woman speaking softly. She sounded as if she were crying, and she kept repeating my name: "Sam, Sam ..."

A sharp voice interrupted.

"Not again! He's alive. This crap has got to stop."